Emerging Voices

American Women Writers

1650–1920

An exhibition held at the Grolier Club, New York

11 March — 2 May 1998

Emerging Voices

ॐ

American
Women Writers
1650–1920

CATALOGUE COMPILED BY
Iola S. Haverstick, Jean W. Ashton, Caroline F. Schimmel, and Mary C. Schlosser

copyright © 1998 by The Grolier Club
ISBN 0-910672-22-9

FRONTISPIECE
John Singleton Copley, *Portrait of Mercy Otis Warren*, c. 1763
(see page 14)

BINDING DECORATION
facsimile of the covers for Celia Thaxter's *An Island Garden*, 1894,
designed by Sarah de St. Prix Wyman Whitman (see page 69)

Designed and typeset in Hightower types by Katy Homans,
and printed by the Stinehour Press.
Hightower type is named for Caroline Hightower,
longtime director of the American Institute of Graphic Arts.

℘ Contents

Phillis Wheatley. Portrait engraved by Scipio Moorhead, c. 1773, for the
frontispiece of her *Poems* (see page 15).
Courtesy The Pierpont Morgan Library, New York. PML 77263.

℘ Introduction

From the earliest colonial beginnings, American women writers have participated in an ongoing effort to record the varieties of experience of settlers and their descendants in the New World. In so doing, these "ink-stained Amazons," as Nathaniel Hawthorne later described them, delineated in their writings many of the major themes that, to one extent or another, were to become staples of American literature. While their initial products today may seem unpolished and often overly didactic imitations of English modes, the writings of these women reflect a sensibility of America which places them in the mainstream of our literary history.

Emerging Voices: American Women Writers attempts to trace the movement of women writers in America from the margins of literary culture and industry to its center. The exhibition explores the substantial canon of works that begins with the homespun verse of Anne Bradstreet, the first volume of poetry published by any American, and closes with the appearance of Edith Wharton's highly polished and sophisticated *Age of Innocence*, winner of the 1921 Pulitzer Prize for the best American novel.

The exhibition is intended as an overview of the works of authors who reflect both the historical concerns of women living in America and the distinctive emerging voice of the American woman writer. The list is not intended to be definitive. Some of the authors in the exhibition are still well-known; others were famous in their own time, but have since been forgotten; still others have been included because of their originality or because of one curator's affection for the author. We were, of course, constrained by the amount of exhibition space available at the Grolier Club. We were also occasionally confounded by the apparent nonexistence of some of the books and manuscripts we would have liked to display, for example, the original manuscript of *The Journal of Madam Knight*, or the first edition of Mary Rowlandson's narrative.

The process of organizing this exhibition has been long and interesting. In the course of discussions and research, commonalities among authors and of themes clamor for more attention than can be given in the necessarily brief labels. Some of these are, upon reflection, not too surprising. For example, minimal biographical research indicated that women who wrote and whose publications reached the marketplace often came from educated families, where as children they had access to libraries and were encouraged to read. Many emerged from what might be called the Sunday School tradition, where the convention of telling stories was supported by custom and the evangelical establishment. One can appreciate all the more the astonishing feat of those who were poorly educated, or whose home "libraries" consisted of a Bible and little else. It is also evident that, for a woman, legal and social strictures until the turn of this century meant writing was one of the few careers available when a husband died or deserted the family. The necessity of entering the economic marketplace and the difficulties encountered with a nearly all-male publishing world turned such writers as Sarah Parton, Mary Abigail Dodge, and Frances Hodgson Burnett into hard-headed business women. Groundwork for the success of writers like Willa Cather and Edith Wharton was thus laid in part by generations of women who quietly fought for the right to enter into contracts and earn a living by their pen.

Since the Grolier Club is organized by and for people who have an abiding interest in books as material objects, the curators would like to acknowledge their pleasure in gathering and putting on public display the actual books and periodicals in which these texts first appeared, as well as a sampling of the original manuscript drafts by these authors. Wherever possible, we have chosen works with inscriptions or autographs, to emphasize the relationship between authors and their public. Few readers today, including the many students who are bringing fresh perspectives to the study of American literature, have the opportunity to see these works as their authors first saw them. Time and loving use have taken their toll, but humble and grand bindings, embellished title pages, and stiff frontispiece portraits all convey important information about literary culture in America.

The original idea for *Emerging Voices*, as well as much of the intellectual content, belongs to Iola S. Haverstick. She asked three other Club members, Jean W. Ashton, Caroline F. Schimmel, and Mary C. Schlosser, to co-curate. We four were helped at a crucial early period by Professor Joan D. Hedrick, Chairman of the Women's Studies Program at Trinity College in Hartford, who made wise suggestions about authors and books. While a portion of the works on view come from the curators' own collections, we are privileged to have been able to count on the generosity of other Club members, friends, and institutions. Eleanor Elliott and Robert H. Jackson have loaned from their private collections. The American Antiquarian Society, Barnard College, the Rare Book and Manuscript Library and the Pulitzer office in the School of Journalism of Columbia University, The Library Company of Philadelphia, the Pierpont Morgan Library, the Museum of Fine Arts, Boston, the New-York Historical Society, the New York Public Library's Rare Books Division and Berg Collection of English and American Literature, the Harriet Beecher Stowe Center, the University of Virginia's Alderman Library, and the Beinecke Library of Yale University have gone out of their way to make their treasures available. Additional thanks must go to Mildred K. Abraham, Georgia B. Barnhill, Virginia L. Bartow, Bud Clement, Ellen Dunlap, Rudolph Ellenbogen, Carol Falcione, H. George Fletcher, Claudia Funke, James M. Green, Margaret Heilbrun, Priscilla Juvelis, Jennifer B. Lee, Robert E. Parks, Rodney Phillips, Michael Plunkett, Jane Randall, Carol Rothkopf, Jane Siegel, Theodore E. Stebbins, Jr., Margaret M. Tamulonis, Ann Thomas, John C. Van Horne, William D. Walker, and Patricia Willis. Essential to our success has been the work of Eric J. Holzenberg, Nancy Houghton, and the Grolier Club staff.

Production of this catalogue was made possible by donations from Jean Ashton, Iola Haverstick, Caroline and Stuart Schimmel, Mary Schlosser, and the Grolier Club.

𝒫𝒶 Voices
in the Wilderness

For nearly 200 years, or until the later part of the eighteenth century, few writings by American women appeared in print. Those which did followed by and large the literary forms popular in England and on the continent, employing the familiar conventions of pious verse and sentimental fiction while trying to convey the less familiar experiences of the New World. In spite of their derivativeness, the best of these works are lively and distinctive, suggesting many of the themes that would appear in women's writing in the centuries to follow.

Anne Bradstreet's verses, for example, while following the conventions set by the metaphysical poets of her era in England, make strong use of domestic detail and the imagery of the family and the hearth. Mary Rowlandson's captivity narrative was, like Bradstreet's poems, not initially published in America. It became the model for countless other tales of the confusing, frightening, but often ambiguous encounters between the indigenous inhabitants of the country and the European émigrés. Sarah Knight's vigorous and amusing account of her 1704 trip from Boston to New York, printed nearly 120 years after it was written, reminds us of how many energetic narratives lie buried within the colonial experience. The cautious introduction to Phillis Wheatley's uncommon poetry makes clear the double burden imposed by race and gender.

Abigail Adams adjured her husband to "remember the ladies" in formulating the laws of the new government. The writings of her close friend, Mercy Otis Warren, embodied one of the ladies' interests that would run through the writings of her female successors until the enactment of the suffrage amendment—a concern for the body politic and a willingness to contend with political and historical issues in print. Susanna Rowson, the new nation's first best-selling novelist, played a contrasting but equally important role. By skillfully packaging melodramas for a growing audience of consumers, she showed a career path that would soon be worn smooth by the many women who also learned their trade along the way.

℘ Anne Dudley Bradstreet
(1612?–1672)

The Tenth Muse Lately Sprung Up in America, or Severall Poems, Compiled With a Great Variety of Wit and Learning . . . By a Gentlewoman in Those Parts.
London: For Stephen Bowtell, 1650
New York Public Library, Rare Books Division

Anne Bradstreet's position as "the mother of American poetry" was the result of the publication, in London in 1650, of *The Tenth Muse*. This earliest "sampler" of the young colonist's verses consisted mainly of Bradstreet's modest embroideries on the poetic modes she had studied before emigrating with her nonconformist parents and husband from England to the Massachusetts Bay Colony in 1630. Both her father Thomas and her husband Simon were governors of the Colony.

Six years after her death, her work was republished as *Several Poems* in Boston. This equally-scarce and anonymous volume, which contains *The Tenth Muse* and much of her more mature and more intimate work, sheds a fascinating light on the Puritan view of life as she experienced it in the Colony. The contemporary American poet Adrienne Rich summed up Bradstreet's achievements: "To have written these, the first good poems in America, while rearing eight children, lying frequently sick, keeping house at the edge of wilderness, was to have managed a poet's range and extension within confines as severe as any American poet has confronted."

ℱℛ Mary White Rowlandson

(ca. 1635–ca. 1678)

*A True History of the Captivity & Restoration of Mrs. Mary
Rowlandson . . .Wherein Is Set Forth the Cruel and Inhumane Usage
She Underwent Amongst the Heathens. . . .*
London: J. Poole, 1682
Caroline F. Schimmel

The vital statistics of the birth and death of Mary Rowlandson,
New England's most famous Indian captive, seem to have been
interred with her, but we do at least know that she was born in
Somersetshire, England, that the family migrated to Salem,
Massachusetts, when she was still a small child, and then moved to
the newly founded "frontier" town of Lancaster, Massachusetts.
There, in 1656, Mary White married the town's first regular parish
minister, Joseph Rowlandson.

On 10 February 1676, during the struggle known as King
Phillip's War, the Wampanaug Indians attacked Lancaster, killing
most of the settlers and taking some twenty-four captives, among
them Mary Rowlandson and her four children. Her husband was
away at the time. Mrs. Rowlandson was later to write in her reminiscences of the ordeal: "I had often before said, that if the Indians
should come, I should chuse rather to be killed by them than taken
alive, but when it came to my tryal my mind changed."

Rowlandson's account, originally written for two of her children who had survived the ordeal with her (a third having died
during the captivity in her mother's arms), was the first published
narrative of a North American Indian captivity. It was widely read
throughout the next hundred or more years and formed the pattern
for a best-selling and sometimes sensational genre that became a
staple of American popular literature. In addition to depicting
details of a woman's life on the New England frontier, Rowlandson's account of the often gruesome details of her captivity also
provides readers with insight into the plight of an uprooted and
often starving native American populace.

The narrative was published the same year in Cambridge, Massachusetts, as *The Soveraignty and Goodness of God.* . . . Both printings claim they are second, "corrected" editions; it is possible there never was a "first," as no copy has been located.

℘ Sarah Kemble Knight
(1666–1727)

The Journals of Madam Knight, and the Rev. Mr. Buckingham. From the Original Manuscripts, Written in 1704 & 1710.
New York: Wilder & Campbell, 1825
Barnard College, Overbury Collection

On 2 October 1704 a Boston shopkeeper and recent widow named Sarah Kemble Knight embarked, alone and on horseback, on an unusual journey which was to result in the first narrative of early frontier travel by an American woman. Written to satisfy the curiosity of her family and friends, not published until 1825, and then only with another early travel narrative, *The Journal of Madam Knight* is regarded today as a classic account of travel and manners, and has been re-issued, complete with idiosyncratic spelling, by three fine printers, as well as in several popular editions.

Sarah Knight's five-month trip from Boston to New York City and back roughly followed the route of the present Amtrak railroad. Although the "Rode," as she referred to it, contained some "Clean . . . and passable" terrain, more often than not, Knight and her guides encountered "swoller rivers," navigable only by canoe or crude ferry, and "Bridges exceeding high and very tottering and of vast length," as well as "steep and Rocky Hills and precipices." Despite these topographical difficulties ("Buggbears to a fearful female travailer"), Madam Knight seems to have kept her equilibrium by masking (and mocking) her difficulties in the numerous asides and in the unexpected bursts of heroic verse which frequently punctuate her *Journal*.

Knight had several very different careers, and must have been an astonishing woman. She conducted a writing school in Boston, and acted as a legal adviser and a recorder of public documents. Moving to Connecticut in 1714, she owned several farms, kept a shop, and speculated in Indian lands.

𝒫ℛ Mercy Otis Warren
(1728–1814)

The Group, A Farce; As Lately Acted, and Re-acted, to the Wonder of All Superior Intelligences.
Boston: Printed, and Sold by Edes and Gill, 1775
Library Company of Philadelphia

History of the Rise, Progress, and Termination of the American Revolution.
Boston: Printed by Manning and Loring, for E. Larkin, 1805.
3 volumes
Barnard College, Overbury Collection

Catalogue frontispiece: John Singleton Copley. *Mrs. James Warren (Mercy Otis).*
Oil on canvas, c. 1763
Bequest of Winslow Warren. Courtesy, The Museum of Fine Arts, Boston

If the title given to Mercy Otis Warren by one of her biographers, "First Lady of the American Revolution," may pretend too much, there can be little doubt that Warren, by virtue of her writings and political connections, nonetheless played a central role in the highly charged events of her times. Born in Barnstable, Massachusetts, the daughter of James Otis, a prosperous farmer-merchant-lawyer and, later, prominent patriot, she was married in 1754 to James Warren, also a leading patriot and member of the state legislature, whose Plymouth home was a meeting place for such proponents of the revolutionary cause as John and Samuel Adams.

As her contribution to the oncoming struggle, Mercy Warren abandoned her earlier poetic efforts in favor of political satires like *The Group*, closet dramas, written to be read, not performed. In the late 1770s she began her monumental *History of the Rise, Progress, and Termination of the American Revolution*, the work upon which her fame chiefly rests. Warren's *History*, which has been recently described as "no less reliable than other histories written during the same era," is still useful today, because of its author's lively opinions and descriptions of persons and events she had known first-hand. It remains a monument to a gallant American female patriot.

℘ Phillis Wheatley,
later
Phillis Wheatley Peters
(1753?-1784)

Poems on Various Subjects, Religious and Moral. By Phillis Wheatley, Negro Servant to Mr. John Wheatley, of Boston, in New England.
London: Printed for A. Bell, Bookseller, and Sold by Messrs. Cox and Barry, Boston, 1773
The Morgan Library copy is signed by the author on the verso of the title page. The portrait was engraved by Scipio Moorhead, a renowned artist and the slave of a Boston minister.
The Pierpont Morgan Library; Barnard College, Overbury Collection

When the eighteen-year-old Phillis Wheatley first submitted her collection of poems for publication, a committee comprised of Boston's most eminent citizens, including Thomas Hutchinson, the governor of Massachusetts, assembled to question her about the authenticity of her work. An Ethiopian brought as a slave to America when she was eight, she had been publishing verse since

1770. Satisfied, the committee composed a brief open letter "To the Publick" stating that, although "under the Disadvantage of serving as a Slave," she had indeed composed the works as written. Because Boston publishers remained incredulous, she and her master's son, Nathaniel Wheatley, traveled to England where they successfully managed to arrange for an edition of the poems to appear. Perhaps coincidentally, she was legally freed the same autumn this book was published.

Wheatley's difficulties exemplified the dilemma faced by American writers who for one reason or another did not fit into orthodox authorial categories. Despite the relative plethora of women printers by the middle of the eighteenth century, only a handful of American women writers had successfully found publishers for their work, and Wheatley, not only a woman but an African-American slave, appeared an oddity both in composing her verses and in seeking to make them public. Until 1829 no other book of imaginative literature in English, written by a black person, male or female, appeared in print.

ৡ Susanna Haswell Rowson
(1762–1824)

Charlotte, A Tale of Truth.
Philadelphia: Printed by D. Humphreys, for M. Carey, 1794
New York Public Library, Rare Book Division

The peripatetic adventures that the multi-talented Susanna Haswell endured during her childhood and adolescence seem more the stuff of fiction than the rather derivative plots of the many popular novels she was later to write. Born in Portsmouth, England, she traveled back and forth between Great Britain, Nova Scotia, and Boston, where her family were interned as Loyalists during the Revolution. After a stage career in England and the colonies, which allowed her to write and produce dramas as well as act, she opened a Young Ladies Academy in Boston, one of America's first schools to offer girls some education beyond the elementary level.

A prolific novelist, as well as the author of plays and text-books, Susanna Rowson's reputation rests largely on her first novel, *Charlotte Temple*, published with that title in London in 1791. A novel of seduction, it is set in part in the new United States, where Charlotte "dies a martyr to the inconstancy of her lover, and the treachery of his friend." Its stilted plot and wooden char-acters may invite ridicule today, but *Charlotte Temple* became American's first "bestseller." Over two hundred editions of the book have since been published.

ᏇᎧ Sarah Sayward Barrell Keating Wood, "Madam Wood"
(1759–1855)

Julia and the Illuminated Baron. A Novel: Founded on Recent Facts, Which Have Transpired in the Course of the Late Revolution of Moral Principles in France. By a Lady of Massachusetts. Portsmouth, NH: Charles Peirce, 1800
The Library Company of Philadelphia

The first-born of eleven children, Sally Barrell lived in relative luxury on the Maine coast for most of her life, first with Judge Sayward, her Loyalist maternal grandfather, and then through two successful marriages. Being well brought up, she turned to writing only during periods of widowhood, to "sweeten many bitter hours." Indeed, she carefully explains in the dedication to *Julia*, "not one social, or one domestic duty, [has] ever been sacri-ficed or postponed by [my] pen." The resulting three novels and several short stories, of which *Julia and the Illuminated Baron* was the first, all involve incredibly sweet, passive heroines who never deserve the roils of action-adventure swirling around them from first page to last. Humbly raised Julia Vallaice (though the farmhouse was equipped with books and a harpsichord), is confronted with disappearing parents, a stolen inheritance, reputed illegitimacy, incestuous propositions, false arrest, smallpox, and kidnapping, before being saved by her true love. The saga is set in France, with forays into Spain. Wood also throws in a trip to America for the same true love to save his cousin and *her* illegitimate child, and to have a providential meeting with the "illustrious Farmer of Mount Vernon," whose slaves amazingly rescue the lad from a shipwreck. The anonymous author repeatedly emphasizes the importance of virtue, while cramming into the plot every human frailty she could, thus making the novel a real page-turner, even today. The poor quality of Wood's local printer's typography and spelling only add to its charm.

ᏸᏖ The Awakening Republic Idealists and Realists

The early decades of the nineteenth century in America were
marked by rapid changes in politics, technology, and the economy.
As the leaders of the Revolutionary period died and the centenary
of George Washington's birth approached, women as well as men
began examining and questioning the high-minded principles of
the Founding Fathers. Following the example of Fanny Wright,
an Englishwoman who founded a colony for freed slaves in Tennessee in 1825 and traveled widely in the United States preaching
the gospel of the socialist Robert Owen, women as diverse in tem-
perament as Lydia Maria Child, Catharine Beecher, the Grimké
sisters, and Margaret Fuller stepped into visible public roles. The
abolitionist movement gained its greatest strength from the work
of women who overcame social strictures and their own scruples
about participating in public affairs to organize meetings and
gather signatures for congressional petitions. The experience they
gained in fighting for a cause, as well as in articulating their opinions in print, would lead eventually and inevitably to a demand
for equal political rights and the vote.

The explosive growth of the newspaper industry in the
nation, aided by the invention of the high speed press, the development of the railroads, and greater literacy, resulted in another
opportunity for women. Newspapers and magazines proliferated.
The new publications required a constant supply of publishable
material suitable for family reading. Educated travelers like
Caroline Kirkland were soon reporting back to an eager female
public on the Eastern seaboard about the sometimes frightening

and sometimes amusing struggles to domesticate nature on the American frontier. Their urban contemporaries, like Lydia Child, wrote about the increasingly crowded cities where poverty was becoming visible and the influx of new immigrant populations was having an impact on the national character. At the same time, the popular success of gift books and literary annuals showed that Americans were eager for the sentimental fiction and poetry provided by such women as the novelist Catharine Sedgwick and poet Lydia Sigourney, the "Sweet Singer of Hartford."

℘ Anne Newport Royall
(1769–1853)

Sketches of History, Life, and Manners in the United States. By a Traveller.
New Haven: Printed for the Author, 1826
Caroline F. Schimmel

The Tennessean.
New Haven: Printed for the Author, 1827
Caroline F. Schimmel

Twenty years after Anne Royall's death, the author of the *Dictionary of American Biography* article tried to explain her "bitter and sarcastic tongue" by stating that she had been kidnapped by Indians as a child and lived with them for fifteen years. As late as 1935, her new *DAB* biographer, Jessica Bridenbaugh, described Royall as "grossly personal, given to tirades against her opponents, and long praises of her benefactors."

Anne Royall was the original muckraker, a completely self-made and unique woman. Thrown into abject poverty as a child, following the death of her father, and again when her wealthy husband died and his will was contested by evil relatives, she developed and maintained an undiminished drive and energy in fighting for numerous righteous causes.

Reared in western Pennsylvania and West Virginia (*not* by Indians), the widowed Royall began to travel in the 1820s, determined to visit every corner of America. When, after a decade of wrangling, her lawsuit concerning Mr. Royall's estate was settled against her, the widow set off to Washington to plead for his pension. With the intervention of John Quincy Adams, she managed to obtain the meager sum of $10 a month. Undaunted, but poor, she turned to writing. *Sketches*, self-published, was her earliest effort. Her travel journals, full of witty observations of America, would produce ten volumes of bumptious prose which, although lacking the polish that a proper education would have ensured, provide lively glimpses of the locales she visited. Her attempt at prose, *The Tennessean*, was once described as "in plot, execution, and character . . . one of the worst works ever written in America." It combines tales of pirates in the Caribbean and fierce Indian attacks with lengthy, if accurate, descriptions of rural life in Tennessee.

Retiring permanently to Washington in 1831, she founded a kitchen-table weekly, *Paul Pry*, later renamed *The Huntress*. In it, she railed against the corruption and complacency of the government. Other targets included slavery, government treatment of the Indians, and the increasingly vocal evangelical movement. Her insults to the latter had earlier resulted in her being convicted and fined as a "common scold," the only such conviction in post-Revolutionary American history.

℘ Catharine Maria Sedgwick
(1789–1867)

Hope Leslie; or, Early Times in the Massachusetts.
New York: Published by White, Gallaher, and White, 1827
Barnard College, Overbury Collection

Married or Single?
New York: Harper & Brothers, 1857
Barnard College, Overbury Collection

Widely hailed as a "founder of American literature" by nineteenth-century critics, as well as by Washington Irving, James Fenimore Cooper, and William Cullen Bryant, Sedgwick's reputation dwindled by the mid-twentieth century to such one line dismissals in surveys of American literature as "purveyor of sentimental romances to genteel females." Actually, contemporary readers (genteel, female, and otherwise) are discovering Sedgwick's unconventional approach to the conventional subject matter of her six novels to be defiant and fresh.

Set, as its title indicates, in seventeenth-century New England, *Hope Leslie*, Sedgwick's third novel, is considered by many critics to be her best. It interweaves a tale of Puritan romance with the darker story of the colonists' subjugation of the native Indian population. While the dominant figures of the novel, Hope Leslie, foster daughter of a prominent Puritan and Magawisca, daughter of a Pequot chief, defy traditional authority (each in the context of her cultural background), at the same time they both display a capacity for selflessness and self-sacrifice, qualities that were increasingly to become hallmarks of the heroines of mid-nineteenth-century American fiction.

Written, according to Sedgwick's preface, to "lessen the stigma placed on the term old maid"—a reflection of its author's lifelong single status—*Married or Single?* was her last and most nearly autobiographical novel. It focuses on the off-and-on courtship between the heroine, who is determined to remain unwed, and her long suffering suitor. Although, the novel's denouement may affront more liberated present-day sensibilities, Sedgwick was a pioneer, attempting to bring a fresh perspective to a prevailing and time-worn assumption of her era.

℘ Lydia Howard Huntley Sigourney
(1791–1865)

Letters to Young Ladies.
Hartford, CT: Printed by P. Canfield, 1833
This copy is inscribed by the author to Matthew Carey, the Irish
radical turned successful Philadelphia publisher. Apparently the
attention-getting gift worked: he produced her *Illustrated Poems*
sixteen years later.
The Library Company of Philadelphia

*Illustrated Poems. With Designs by Feliz O.C. Darley, Engraved by
American Artists.*
Philadelphia: Carey and Hart, 1849
Yale University, Beinecke Library

*Autograph letter, signed, to Dolly (Mrs. James) Madison, 26 August
1825.*
As part of her thank-you note to her hostess, after visiting the
former president and his wife at their farm in Virginia, Sigourney
composed this lyrical poem, "Montpelier."
New York Public Library, Berg Collection of English and American Literature

From seemingly humble beginnings—she was born in Norwich,
Connecticut, where her father was a hired man in the household
of a wealthy Norwich widow—Lydia Sigourney parlayed her
opportunities and talents into a successful career as a writer of
both essays and poetry. After a stint as a school mistress and principal, she opted in 1819 for marriage to Charles Sigourney, then a
well-to-do merchant. Shortly thereafter, she began selling her
early poems and sketches to the popular magazines of the day.
The success of these various productions, combined with her husband's declining prosperity, persuaded Sigourney to pursue literature as a trade. During her most productive period, roughly from
1840 to 1850, she published fourteen volumes which have been
described by a biographer as mostly "a reshuffling of her earlier

work." Nonetheless, her combination of themes of domesticity and comparisons of flowers to female sensibilities, which today seem almost unbearably cloying, caused her to be acclaimed as "the Sweet Singer of Hartford." The *Letters to Young Ladies* was already in its fourteenth edition in 1845. Summing up her own writings in later life, Sigourney noted: "If there is any kitchen in Parnassus, my Muse has surely officiated there as a woman of all work and an aproned waiter." Though posterity has sustained Sigourney's candid appraisal of her *oeuvre*, the fact remains that she was one of the first American women to achieve a successful literary career. Because of her stature, it distressed many when in the 1850s she blithely dismissed the women's rights movement, having always considered politics unfeminine.

℘ Sarah Moore Grimké
(1792–1873)

℘ Angelina Emily Grimké,
later

Mrs. Theodore Dwight Weld
(1805–1879)

An Appeal to the Christian Women of the South. By A. E. Grimké.
[New York or London?]: American Anti-Slavery Society, 1836
First edition.
The Library Company of Philadelphia

An Appeal to the Christian Women of the South. By A. E. Grimké.
[New York?]: American Anti-Slavery Society, 1836
Third Edition, "Revised and Corrected." To this copy the author has added in pen, below her printed signature at the end, "Shrewsbury, N. J., 1836. Third edition. Angelina Grimké."
University of Virginia, Special Collections

While the South for the most part slept, basking in the sunset of an antebellum society, two courageous South Carolina sisters were busy in the North preaching the gospels of abolition and woman suffrage. Raised Presbyterian, in a slave milieu, and taught only the household arts, these two Grimké sisters managed to grow up utterly unlike their other siblings and neighbors. Self-taught secretly from reading her father's law books, Sarah left for Philadelphia "to escape the sound of the driver's lash and the shrieks of the tortured victims [of slavery]." Her much younger sister soon followed. There they were accepted as ministers in the Quaker faith, and joined its abolitionist and suffragist causes.

The first of the sisters to appear in print was the more extroverted Angelina, whose abolitionist pamphlet, *An Appeal to the Christian Women of the South*, was published in 1836 by the fledgling American Anti-Slavery Society. She begged her former neighbors and friends to stop this crime against God and man. The reaction was dramatic: postmasters below the Mason-Dixon line destroyed copies of the pamphlet and Angelina was warned never to return to Charleston. In the same year, and under the same imprint, Sarah Grimké's equally angry *Epistle to the Clergy of the Southern States* was published, assuring the sisters a well-deserved place in the pantheon of the abolitionist movement. Angelina's 1837 *Letters to Catharine E. Beecher* again took issue with slavery.

Sarah Grimké, described later as less handsome and charming than her sister, but just as pious, saw the legal degradation of women to be as wrong as the enslavement of African-Americans, and just as contrary to the teachings of the Bible. Her 1838 *Letters* was the first pamphlet on women's rights to be published in America. Both sisters were an oddity in the North—plain of dress, lilting yet fiery of speech, attracting audiences of working people to public lectures through the 1830s. But soon the church hierarchy, and such male abolitionists as John Greenleaf Whittier, accused them of drawing women away from their "natural" familial sphere. They were publicly chastised in Philadelphia, and then in Massachusetts. The two of them, together with newly-wed Angelina's husband, Theodore Weld, published one last salvo, *American Slavery As It Is*, in 1839, before they virtually disappeared from view. Yet, their lives were full. They were mentors to young Elizabeth Cady Stanton. They would raise and support two illegitimate half-black nephews, one of whom became the first black man to graduate from Harvard Law School and the other, a Princeton graduate, would marry Charlotte Forten. Their impact on future generations of critical thinkers, especially on Stanton and Harriet Beecher Stowe, would be undeniable.

℘⌇ Sarah Josepha Buell Hale
(1788–1879)

Northwood, a Tale of New England. By a Lady of New Hampshire.
Boston: Published by Bowles & Dearborn; Ingraham & Hewes, Printers, 1827. 2 volumes
This copy has a presentation inscription from the author to Baron Stow, a New Hampshire Baptist clergyman who moved to Boston in 1832. He was active in the church until 1867, and published several books on religion.
New York Public Library, Berg Collection of English and American Literature

The Ladies' Magazine, Conducted by Mrs. Sarah J. Hale.
[Volume 1.]
Boston: Published by Putnam & Hunt, 1828
This set was bought new by the printer Isaiah Thomas for $3.50. He had the year's issues bound together, inserting as a frontispiece the engraving of the locally well-regarded, if eccentric, professional

researcher and writer Hannah Adams, and gave it to the American Antiquarian Society in 1829.

American Antiquarian Society

Poems for Our Children. Designed for Families, Sabbath Schools, and Infant Schools. Written to Inculcate Moral Truths and Virtuous Sentiments. Part the First [all published].
Boston: Marsh, Capen & Lyon, 1830
New York Public Library, Rare Book Division

Pregnant with her fifth child, the suddenly-bereaved Sarah Hale turned to writing. A slender volume of poems was published (subsidized by her late husband's Masonic Temple), aptly titled *The Genius of Oblivion.* Four years later came her first novel, *Northwood*, weak on plot, but filled with pious preaching and details of daily life in her Yankee New England. It was so well received that she moved the family to Boston, where she founded a periodical to reflect her refined, genteel taste, *The Ladies' Magazine.* The first periodical aimed at the female market to last more than five years, with Hale at the editorial helm, it would actually thrive until 1877, and survive until 1898, through her move to Philadelphia with the merger with Louis Godey's failing *Lady's Book,* and several name changes. A powerful voice addressed to the female middle class eager to be fashionable, the periodical was rich in advice and fold-out colored plates depicting all aspects of deportment. Among her co-editors was Lydia Sigourney, and among her contributors were Caroline Hentz, Caroline Kirkland, Sara Lippincott, Emma Southworth, and Harriet Beecher Stowe. It managed to be so firmly a high-brow publication that there was never any mention of the Civil War.

Like Sigourney a proponent of "ideal femininity," Sarah Hale carefully toed the line of social acceptability. The woman whose dainty anti-intellectual pose so rankled Elizabeth Cady Stanton that the feminist would practically sputter actually led a fascinating double life. An extraordinarily energetic person, and a powerful literary and political voice, she was an early advocate for girls' education, for female doctors, and for the rights of married and working women. She was also instrumental in making Thanksgiving a national holiday.

In yet another persona, Hale's slim work, *Poems for Our Children*, while at the time so poorly received that there was never a *Part the Second*, is considered an icon of American literature today, containing, as it does, "Mary Had a Little Lamb." The ode first appeared the same year in an issue of the *Juvenile Miscellany*, under her initials, but received nationwide attention only when chosen to appear in *McGuffey's Second Reader* in 1857. Meanwhile, apparently to capture the growing abolitionist reading public, Child revised and reissued *Northwood* in 1852, giving it a timely new title, *Northwood; or, Life North And South, Showing the True Character of Both*. Though the few references to the South in the original novel were only to emphasize the Puritan industriousness of the Northern post-colonial character, in hindsight one could see her emphasizing the economic conflicts which would inevitably result in the Civil War.

℘ The Lowell Offering

The Lowell Offering for October, 1840. Written, Edited and Published by Female Operatives Employed in the Mills.
Lowell, MA: Printed by A. Watson, 1840 [and by others, 1841–45]
Barnard College, Overbury Collection

The effects of industrialization in America were strongly felt in the early decades of the nineteenth century as factories began to open in rural areas where cheap water power made manufacturing feasible. The woolen mills in Lowell, Massachusetts, were only one industry among many that attracted young women, offering them salaries that could supplement the often meager proceeds of family farms or small town businesses.

Concern with conditions in the mills and the living situations of the displaced employees was widespread. In Lowell, the young female operatives were encouraged to meet "to read aloud their literary creations" in "Improvement Circles." In October 1840, the first number of *The Lowell Offering*, a compilation of these writings, was published. Harriet Jane Hanson, the editor, verifying that the productions were original to the factory women, points out to readers of this first issue, "In estimating the talent of the writers for *The Offering*, the fact should be remembered, that they are actively employed in the Mills for more than twelve hours out of every twenty four. The evening, after 8 o'clock," she continues, "affords their only opportunity for composition; and whoever will consider the sympathy between mind and body, must be sensible that a day of constant manual employment, even though the labor be not excessive, must in some measure unfit the individual for the full developement [*sic*] of mental power."

The Lowell Offering was published for five years. Whether exhaustion of the operatives or the nascent trade union movement caused its demise is not entirely clear. "Leaves, by a Dreamer," "Return of Spring," "Ramble of Imagination," "Hill Side and Fountain Rill"—the romantic titles (and content) of many of the stories and poems suggest that the young women were entirely at home with the conventions of the gift books and annuals so popular at the time. Other articles suggest that the men who subsidized it encouraged positive thinking about factory life: "Ambition and Contentment," "Pleasures of Factory Life," "Aristocracy of Employment," and "Flowers in the Mills."

℘ Catharine Esther Beecher
(1800–1878)

A Treatise on Domestic Economy, for the Use of Young Ladies at Home, and at School.
Boston: Marsh, Capen, Lyon, and Webb, 1841
Mary C. Schlosser

Autograph letter to her publisher, Harper & Brothers, 19 December 1855. Beecher encloses with the letter a group of drawings for her new book, *Physiology and Calisthenics for Schools and Families,* which she readily admits are copied from another artist's work: "I think any lawyer will tell you that in drawing from objects that must be alike—such as single bones of the body, no damages can be claimed for copy right." The Morgan Library also owns the incredulous, nearly hysterical response from the publisher.

The Pierpont Morgan Library, New York (MA 1950)

Catharine Beecher devoted her life to women's education and social reform. The oldest of the thirteen children of Calvinist minister Lyman Beecher, Catharine attended Sarah Pierce's Litchfield Female Academy in Connecticut. When Alexander Fisher, the Yale mathematics professor to whom she was engaged, drowned in a shipwreck in 1822, her father pronounced him damned as he had not "converted." The emotional and religious turmoil this caused would color Catharine's thinking for the rest of her life. In 1823, the disconsolate spinster turned to work, opening a girls' school in Hartford, where she was assisted in teaching by her sisters Mary and Harriet.

She moved with her father and other family members to Cincinnati in 1832. She opened the first of several teacher-training schools, the Western Female Institute. There, despite the ill health which was a continuing concern throughout her life, she began a career of writing, speaking, and traveling to raise money to support her schools and other enterprises.

Besides essays and poems, Catharine produced religious, political, and philosophical works. As early as 1829, her *Suggestions on Education* for girls' schools gave her national exposure in print. *A Treatise on Domestic Economy* won instant recognition as a valuable guide to homemaking, covering every aspect from building a house to setting up an efficient kitchen. The introductory chapters outline Beecher's philosophy that woman's importance in society lies in her responsibility for educating the family and creating the moral tone necessary for maintaining a democratic and Christian nation. There are chapters on health and general first aid, cooking, cleanliness, exercise, manners, charity and money management, the raising of children, sewing, gardening, and much more. By

1843, it was in its fourth printing, and was reprinted almost every year until 1856, giving Catharine some financial security after years of impecuniousness.

Unlike her younger siblings, Harriet, Henry Ward Beecher, and Isabella Beecher Hooker, Catharine was a vigorous opponent of the woman suffrage movement, asserting that women should influence society through moral training in the home and that opportunities for higher education and employment were more important than the vote.

℘ Caroline Matilda Stansbury Kirkland, "Mary Clavers"
(1801–1864)

A New Home—Who'll Follow? or, Glimpses of Western Life. By Mrs. Mary Clavers, an Actual Settler.
New York: C. S. Francis; Boston: J. H. Francis, 1839
Caroline F. Schimmel

A first-person account of its Eastern-bred author's stay, with her husband and their young children, in a remote Michigan settlement from, roughly, 1837 to 1842, *A New Home* was Kirkland's first and most popular book. The novel incorporates, in the words of a recent critic, "the conventions of travel literature, autobiography, satire, criticism, and domestic fiction." Omitted from this summary is that Kirkland's caustic and often biting descriptions of what she perceived to be the vulgarity of all her frontier neighbors, have come to overshadow the realistic content of an historically important and entertaining record of an early "western" settlement. Her statement that women would suffer much more than men from being torn from "her own dear fire-side" for this rough existence, was the first printed warning in an otherwise optimistic stream of (male) accounts of the wondrous frontier lands. The book would be reprinted in America and England, was in its tenth edition by 1850, and is still in print today.

Elizabeth Palmer Peabody
(1804–1894)

Mary Tyler Peabody Mann, Mrs. Horace Mann
(1806–1887)

The Moral Culture of Infancy, & Kindergarten Guide.
Boston: T. O. H. P. Burnham, 1863
American Antiquarian Society

Throughout her life, Elizabeth Peabody's major interest was the development and education of young children, a calling no doubt inspired in her childhood by her mother, who ran a school in Salem, Massachusetts, and believed "that every child should be treated as a genius." Elizabeth started a school of her own in 1822 in Boston, where she met Ralph Waldo Emerson, William Ellery Channing, and Bronson Alcott. She later became Alcott's assistant in his experimental school. Through her equally bright if much less assertive sisters Sophia and Mary, she was sister-in-law to Nathanial Hawthorne and public school advocate Horace Mann. In 1840 she opened a bookshop in Boston that became a center for the Transcendental movement, whose meetings were led by Margaret Fuller. The bookshop was ultimately unsuccessful, and after it closed in 1850, Elizabeth traveled and lectured widely, promoting early education, abolition, and social reform.

By 1859 she had begun to encourage the establishment of "kindergartens" (based on the concept of pre-school as a "children's garden" developed two decades earlier in Germany by Friedrich Froebel), and in 1860 founded the first such school in America. From then on, often assisted by her sister Mary, she dedicated her energies to promoting early childhood education. Her most important book, *Moral Culture*, was written in collaboration with Mary, who had long been involved in her husband's crusade to rethink public education. Current teaching, especially in Boston schools, was still based on the belief that all children were innately evil. The sisters' book deals with the connections between the kindergarten movement and the romantic, idealistic, and individualistic beliefs of Transcendentalism. In it they maintained that the ideals of self-reliance and individualism would be nurtured in children in these schools. Elizabeth continued an arduous life of writings and lectures into a vigorous old age. She is said to be the model for Miss Birdseye in Henry James's *The Bostonian*.

Sarah Margaret Fuller, Marchesa d' Ossoli, "Margaret Fuller"
(1810–1850)

Summer On the Lakes, in 1843. By S. M. Fuller.
Boston: C. C. Little and J. Brown, 1844
This issue of the first edition includes seven sepia etched plates by the author.
Caroline F. Schimmel

Woman in the Nineteenth Century. By S. Margaret Fuller.
New York: Greeley & McElrath; W. Osborn, printer, 1845
This copy from the library of the English traveler and author, Fanny Kemble Butler, with her signature and bookplate.
University of Virginia, C. Waller Barrett Collection

"I am determined on distinction," a precocious Margaret Fuller announced to her school headmistress while still in her teens. And while Fuller's reputation, both during her prime and following her premature death (with her Italian husband, Angelo Ossoli, and their two-year-old son in a shipwreck off Fire Island in 1850), has seesawed between ridicule and near-cult status, the distinction she craved continues to focus on her commanding personality and on her unconventional and ultimately tragic personal history. Thus, while there has been no shortage of Fuller biographies, access to her writings on which her literary reputation primarily rests, has been limited until recently to ageing first editions on library shelves.

Fuller's first book-length attempt at "distinction" records a voyage undertaken in the summer of 1843 with her friends Sarah and James Freeman Clarke, to visit various of their respective relatives who had settled in "the West." Following a passage by steamer through the Great Lakes to Chicago, a city of some 8,000, the travelers proceeded by covered wagon to the prairie village of Oregon, Illinois, to which a Fuller uncle had migrated in the 1820s. Fuller's idealistic expectations of experiencing the building of a "New Eden in the wilderness" and her subsequent disillusionment parallel those of earlier nineteenth-century female travelers, such as Caroline Kirkland in *A New Home*. Present-day scholars have noted that her book suffers from insistent digressions and subjective meanderings. Nonetheless, although far from a bestseller, *Summer on the Lakes* was sufficiently well-received by Fuller's contemporaries to warrant a second printing.

Fuller's *Woman in the Nineteenth Century* has been widely acknowledged in the twentieth century as a major document of American feminism. It is something of an anomaly that the treatise for which Fuller is most renowned should have first appeared in print in 1845 as part of a series which the publishers had euphemistically (at least, in Fuller's case) labeled "Useful Books for the People." Decidedly more polemical than practical, *Woman in the Nineteenth Century* is an expansion of an article entitled "The Great Lawsuit: Man *versus* Man, Woman *versus* Woman," which Fuller had published in the Transcendentalist magazine *The Dial* in 1843. The subject of both works, not surprisingly, is the inferior status of women in the new American republic and the possibilities for future equality of the sexes, with "every path laid open to woman as freely as to man." Once again Fuller allowed the intensity of her emotions and her penchant for free association to intrude on her message and there was no other edition during her lifetime.

✌ The Power of Words
Women and Politics

The immediate and unprecedented success of Harriet Beecher
Stowe's impassioned plea for the abolition of slavery, originally
advertised, though not ultimately published as *Uncle Tom's Cabin,
or, The Man That Was a Thing*, should have suggested to any male
readers who might have remained skeptical that women writers
were capable of exploiting the uses of the press quite as effectively
as men. Stowe's novel, inspired by abolitionist rhetoric and religious conviction, highlighted the bitter and tragic contradictions
of a social philosophy which sanctioned, in slavery, the violation
of chastity and family ties. Indeed, such fiction could be more
effective than fact, when as in Stowe's case, the superior moral
sensitivity and religious feeling usually attributed to women could
be harnessed to the cause of political reform. Literary responses to
Uncle Tom's Cabin by women were as varied and passionate as
those of men. Publishers supporting abolition sought out reminiscences of former slaves. From the South came ardent defenses
of the status quo, like Caroline Hentz's feverish justification of
the slave system in *The Planter's Northern Bride*. Harriet Wilson's
Our Nig, one of the earliest novels to describe the difficult lives of
free black people in New England, showed another aspect of the
struggle.

The idea that a novel might move its readers to action was not
new, but for women, who were less likely than men to speak out
in public, fiction and (sometimes fictionalized) autobiography
were often the only ways to expose social grievances, enlist support for public causes, or articulate moral concerns. Although a
disgruntled Nathaniel Hawthorne decried the products of the
"scribbling women" whose books appeared to be flooding the market, these sentimental writings were astonishingly effective in

reaching other female readers and in mobilizing through them the fathers, husbands, and sons who enjoyed direct political power.

A goodly number of illustrious female writers, including Catharine Beecher and Mary Abigail Dodge, firmly opposed extending the franchise to women. Yet women began to heed the Grimké sisters' overtly political speeches and pamphlets questioning the lack of women in the political process. And in these middle years of the century, Susan B. Anthony and Elizabeth Cady Stanton would gather and focus the groundswell of women's, and men's, new perceptions of suffrage that would culminate in the passage of the Nineteenth Amendment only a year before the publication of Wharton's *The Age of Innocence*.

৪৯ Lydia Maria Francis Child
(1802–1880)

Hobomok. A Tale of Early Times, By an American.
Boston: Published by Cummins, Hilliard & Co., Printed by Hilliard & Metcalf, 1824
This copy has a presentation inscription from Mrs. Child to Maria Edgeworth, the Irish author of novels, tales for young people, and advice on raising children.
University of Virginia, C. Waller Barrett Collection

An Appeal in Favor of That Class of Americans Called Africans.
Boston: Allen and Ticknor, 1833
New York Public Library, Berg Collection of English and American Literature

Lydia Maria Francis, one of six children of a prosperous baker in Medford, Massachusetts, opted early for a literary career. Before she was twenty-five, she had founded the first American children's periodical, *Juvenile Miscellany*, and had written two successful novels. One of these, *Hobomok*, an historical romance based on the love between a white woman and an American Indian, earned her entrée to the prestigious library of the Boston Athenaeum. After she married abolitionist lawyer David Lee Child, despite the objections of her family, she was converted to the anti-slavery cause. Five years later she produced *An Appeal in Favor of That Class of Americans Called Africans*, a tract which not only cogently outlined the arguments against slavery, but also gave an overview of African customs and the history of slavery. It also revealed her unconventional views on interracial marriage. The first anti-slavery document ever published, it stunned Boston. The *Juvenile Miscellany* collapsed. Her Athenaeum privileges were withdrawn and she was ostracized by Boston society.

Undaunted by these reversals, Child persisted in both her anti-slavery and literary efforts. Although the latter, a potpourri of various literary genres designed to cater to the popular tastes of the day, never achieved the success of her earlier works, she nonetheless has been designated as "one of America's first women of letters." Apart from her abolitionist writings, her best known work today is "Thanksgiving Day," which begins "Over the river and through the wood, to grandfather's [*sic*] house we go."

𝆏 Harriet Beecher Stowe
(1811–1896)

Original manuscript of "Uncle Tom's Cabin," Chapter 1, pp. 24–25. These two (of the few known) pages from the manuscript show very much a work in process. Written to weekly deadlines, with many changes and deletions, most of the manuscript was discarded by the newspaper's printer, as was then common practice, which Stowe would rue in later years
Mary C. Schlosser

"Uncle Tom's Cabin."
National Era, Washington, DC, 5 June 1851–1 April 1852
Harriet Beecher Stowe Center, Hartford

Uncle Tom's Cabin; or, Life Among the Lowly.
Boston: John P. Jewett & Company; Cleveland, Ohio: Jewett,
Proctor & Worthington, 1852. 2 volumes
Both the plain and the "gift" issue are displayed.
Mary C. Schlosser

The Minister's Wooing.
New York: Derby and Jackson, 1859
Mary C. Schlosser

Autograph letter, signed H B Stowe, 11 May 1874.
Stowe is writing to an autograph seeker named Mr. Fisher, who
requests a page from *Uncle Tom*. Not having thought to retrieve
the manuscript from the printers at the time, "Now I would give a
pretty sum for it but it is asking for last year's leaves." She encloses a page from an article, apologising that she is not as "methodi-
cal as Mrs. Lewes [George Eliot] who writes in books & whose
manuscripts stand side by side of her printed works as trimly
bound volumes."
Mary C. Schlosser

The seventh of the thirteen children of Lyman Beecher, Stowe
was, like her sister Catharine, deeply influenced by religious philosophy. At the age of thirteen, she went to Hartford to study and
teach at Catharine's Hartford Female Seminary. In 1832 she moved
with much of the family to Cincinnati, where her father would
head Lane Theological Seminary.

Temporarily relieved from the duties of school mistress, she
wrote a children's geography text and some short stories. As the
child and then spouse of a poorly paid clergyman, Harriet was
from the first grateful for the monetary rewards of writing. Calvin
Stowe, whom she wed in 1836, was a professor at her father's
Seminary, and so steeped in biblical scholarship that he had little
financial ambition, yet he proudly encouraged her to become a
"literary woman." During the 1830s and 1840s, Stowe's stories
began to appear regularly in such periodicals as *Godey's Lady's*

Book, and her first anthology was published in 1843. In the years that followed, she polished her writing skills whenever motherhood (she bore seven children), housework, and frequent ill health permitted.

Residence in Cincinnati, a border town of the free state of Ohio, across the river from the slave state of Kentucky, had exposed Harriet to all the dichotomies of freedom and slavery. Her family and many New England friends had long been abolitionists. The 1850 passage of the Fugitive Slave Law, with its $10 bounty for escaped slaves and $1,000 fine and prison term for anyone assisting the runaways, led to turmoil in Ohio as free blacks and fugitives alike were seized. The Beecher and Stowe families were instantly radicalized. Though Harriet and her growing family left for Brunswick, Maine, that year, when Calvin became a professor at Bowdoin College, she was asked to supply some articles for an abolitionist newspaper, the *National Era*. She planned to submit a series of only three or four sketches, but, as she wrote to weekly deadlines with inflamed emotions, "Uncle Tom's Cabin" poured forth. The following March, just before the appearance of the last installment, the work was published in two volumes. As was routine at the time, the novel was sold in both a regular and a "gift" binding, the latter a very successful merchandising ploy in this era of poetry albums and remembrance tokens. By the end of the summer, more than 100,000 copies had been sold. It was a world-wide bestseller and, with no international copyright in effect, more than thirty pirated editions and translations were already in print in Europe by the end of 1852.

In *Uncle Tom's Cabin* Stowe applied her perceptions of human nature to blacks and whites in equal measure. The poignancy of the narrative, often sentimental or melodramatic, allows to slaves and to their owners the same depth of emotion, thereby demonstrating the depravity of slavery as an institution. Its effectiveness as a tool for the abolitionist cause would be hard to exaggerate. In addition to having an international impact, it served as the literary model for future authors with political agendas, such as Helen

Hunt Jackson. For the rest of her life, based on the success of this, her first novel, Stowe was an accepted fixture in the literary world. She stopped writing only in 1883, having produced scores of novels, travel books, periodical essays, fiction, and children's stories.

Perhaps her most successful later work was *The Minister's Wooing*. In this novel of redemption, the heroine Mary Scudder rejects her suitor, James Marvyn, for his lack of religious faith. He goes to sea and is reported dead in a shipwreck, but later reappears, having been converted by his miraculous survival. After a number of plot complications, the couple are happily married. Written from the remembered anguish of Harriet's sister Catharine, whose fiancé had perished in an 1822 shipwreck, and the fresh pain of her own son Henry's drowning at age nineteen, the novel offers consolation and hope of salvation. It transmutes the stern and rigid theology of her father's Calvinism into a more merciful and optimistic religious belief. The audience for such themes was large (astonishingly, one of the nineteenth-century authors in this exhibition and three of their husbands died at sea) and included the many families of those who had died in the Civil War.

℘ Caroline Lee Hentz
(1800–1856)

The Planter's Northern Bride. A Novel. With Illustrations from Original Designs.
Philadelphia: Parry & M'Millan, 1854
Mary C. Schlosser

Another breadwinner who wrote to augment the income of her ailing husband, a French etymologist and university professor, Hentz wrote short stories for *Godey's Lady's Book*, a popular play, and a number of commercially successful romantic novels, including the 1833 *Lovell's Folly*, which was suppressed by her family as too personal. New England born, she spent her adult life in North

Carolina and Kentucky. *The Planter's Northern Bride* and her other bestseller, *Marcus Warland* (1852), though long since forgotten, were among the most effective of the many attacks on Stowe's abolitionist work. *Northern Bride* was reprinted twice in Philadelphia that year, including an apparent piracy by T. B. Peterson. While defending the religion and morality of the South, Hentz did incorporate in the novels myriad interesting details of plantation life.

𝕱ᴧ Harriet E. Adams Wilson
(ca. 1825/8–ca. 1870)

Our Nig; or, Sketches from the Life of a Free Black, in a Two-Story White House, North, Showing that Slavery's Shadows Fall Even There. By "Our Nig."
Boston: Printed by Geo. C. Rand & Avery, 1859
Columbia University, Rare Book and Manuscript Library

The few facts known about Harriet Wilson are gleaned from federal census records and local town records of marriage, birth, and the county farm (or poor house). Born Harriet Adams, she is recorded in 1850 as living in Milford, New Hampshire, with a white family as a bound servant. In 1851 she married a free black man, Thomas Wilson. Within a year she had been abandoned by her husband, and bore a son, George Mason Wilson, at the poorhouse in Goffstown, New Hampshire. From 1855 to 1863, city records show that she was living in Boston. She suffered from poor health, brought on by overwork in her youth, and was unable to support herself as a housekeeper after her husband's departure. Her novel, *Our Nig*, was written in an attempt to raise enough money to reclaim her seven-year-old son from a foster home, but he died only a few months after its publication, before they could be reunited. Much of the biographical information beyond the public documents comes from three letters printed in an appendix to her book, which endorse her novel and describe the author's life. Further details can perhaps be deduced from the novel itself.

Probably the first novel by an African American published in the United States, *Our Nig* is a semi-autobiographical account of a free black woman's efforts to earn a living and raise a child in a northern setting, where the prejudices of white society could not be overcome. In *Our Nig*, a white woman is married to a black man and abandoned by him. The orphaned mulatto child of this union, Frado, tries to earn her living as an indentured servant in a Northern white household, where she is cruelly abused. Frado briefly achieves independence as a milliner, marries an escaped slave, has a child, and is abandoned by her husband. She and the child are left homeless.

Wilson "openly anticipated a hostile reaction to her text from anti-slavery forces . . . her book is not about the horrors of slavery in the South, but about the horrors of racism in the North," according to historian Henry Louis Gates, Jr. in his 1993 essay in *Black Women in America*. Having dared to write about mixed marriage and Northern racism—two subjects unacceptable to even the "liberal" abolitionists—the author and her grim, hypnotic tale disappeared from view for nearly a century and a half.

℘ Harriet Ann Jacobs, "Linda Brent"
(1813–1897)

Incidents in the Life of a Slave Girl, Written by Herself.
Boston: Published for the Author, 1861
The Library Company of Philadelphia

Born into slavery in North Carolina in 1813, Harriet Jacobs gave birth to two children, fathered by a white slaveholder, before she was twenty. Continually harassed and sexually threatened by her white owner (not the father of her children), she escaped. However, she was forced to hide for nearly seven years in the loft of her (free) grandmother's house, in an uninsulated space under the roof only three feet high, less than a hundred yards from her persecutor's home. When she finally managed to leave Edenton, she suffered still more because, as a fugitive slave, she could at any time be betrayed and returned to her master.

Encouraged by abolitionists to write her almost incredible story, Jacobs finally gained the patronage of Lydia Maria Child, who edited her work and helped her find a publisher. When two publishers in succession went bankrupt before the book could appear, Jacobs managed to purchase the stereotype plates herself and 2,000 copies were printed. A London edition from the same plates followed. Because of its vivid writing and shocking content, Jacob's book has become a widely studied text.

℘ Charlotte L. Forten,
later
Mrs. Francis James Grimké
(1837–1914)

"Life on the Sea Islands."
Atlantic Monthly, Vol. 13, May and June, 1864
Mary C. Schlosser

Charlotte Forten was born into a prosperous free middle-class black family in Philadelphia, and enjoyed a privileged childhood. She was taught by private tutors until she was sent to Salem, Massachusetts, in 1854 to complete her education. After graduating from Salem Normal School, she was appointed as the first African-American teacher in the Epes Grammar School in Salem.

In 1862, on the recommendation of the abolitionist and poet John Greenleaf Whittier, whom she had come to know in Salem, she was sent to St. Helena Island, South Carolina, to participate in the Fort Royal experiment. Alongside a number of white Northern teachers, she worked on a project designed to prove that ex-slaves could be educated, trained as soldiers, and become responsible citizens. "Life on the Sea Islands" was based on the letters about this experience that she sent to Whittier, who arranged for their publication in the *Atlantic Monthly*.

Two years later, she moved to Washington, D.C., where she met and married, in 1878, a Princeton graduate, Francis Grimké, the son of a slave and a southern planter who was the brother of Sarah and Angelina Grimké. Charlotte continued to write essays and sentimental poetry and to devote her life to abolition and other social causes. She suffered from bouts of tuberculosis from her youth, and was an invalid from 1887 until her death.

Her most important writings are contained in five manuscript diaries dating from 1854 to 1864 and 1885 to 1892, which give vivid descriptions of what life was like for an educated black woman of her time. The *Journals* are preserved with her papers at Howard University in Washington, and were first published in 1953.

℘ Elizabeth Cady Stanton
(1815–1902)

Eighty Years and More (1815–1897). Reminiscences of Elizabeth Cady Stanton.
New York: European Publishing Company, 1898
This copy is inscribed by the author to Francis Torrey Morton, on 12 June 1901: "The few have no right to the luxuries of life, while the many are denied its necessities."
Caroline F. Schimmel

If Elizabeth Cady Stanton had not existed, surely some modern-day feminist historian would by now have invented her. One hundred and fifty years after that pivotal July convocation in Seneca Falls, her life would seem to provide a role model for contemporary women. Born in Johnstown, New York, the eldest of five daughters (her older brother died when she was eleven) of a distinguished lawyer who served in Congress and as a Justice of the New York Supreme Court, Stanton initially studied Greek at home and, subsequently, Latin and mathematics at Johnstown Academy. She graduated in 1832 from Emma Willard's Troy Female Seminary, then only a fashionable finishing school. An instinctive reformer, Elizabeth Cady soon became involved in the abolitionist movement. Through a cousin, she met and wed, in 1840, Henry Brewster Stanton, a Boston journalist and outstanding spokesman for the anti-slavery cause, with whom she would have seven children. The word "obey" was, at her insistence, omitted from the marriage ceremony. With his encouragement, she would meet Lucretia Mott, the Grimké sisters, and younger feminists including Susan B. Anthony, who was to become her close friend.

Shortly after moving with her ill husband and growing family from Boston to Seneca Falls, New York, Mrs. Stanton and three of her followers organized the first woman's rights convention, which met on 19 July 1848, in Seneca Falls. Here she formally proposed the first resolution to openly call for woman suffrage, a cause for which she was to campaign unceasingly during the remaining fifty-four years of her life. In addition to writing numerous magazine and newspaper articles, Stanton prepared, with Susan B. Anthony, the initial three volumes of the monumental *History of Woman Suffrage*, covering the years 1848 to 1875. The year that Stanton turned eighty-three, she published her reminiscences as *Eighty Years and More*. She died in her sleep three years later, just after she had fired off a letter to President Theodore Roosevelt urging his support for woman suffrage.

ৡৡ Susan Brownell Anthony
(1820–1906)

ৡৡ Ida Husted Harper
(1851–1931)

History of Woman Suffrage. Edited by Elizabeth Cady Stanton, Susan B. Anthony, and Matilda Joslyn Gage. [Vol. 4: Susan B. Anthony and Ida Husted Harper; Vols. 5–6: Ida Husted Harper.] Illustrated with Steel Engravings. In Two [i.e., Six] Volumes.
New York: Fowler & Wells, Publishers, 1887; Vols. 2–3: Rochester, NY: Susan B. Anthony, Charles Moon; London & Paris: G. Fischbacker, 1887; Vol. 4: Rochester, NY: Susan B. Anthony, 1902; Vols. 5–6: New York: National American Woman Suffrage Association, 1922
These copies of Volumes 2 and 3 are inscribed to "Miss Lilian Whiting, With the admiration of her sincere friend Susan B. Anthony. Rochester, N. Y. July 4, 1888." Whiting was then a young Bostonian author and friend of Sarah Orne Jewett. She later wrote several charming accounts of her travels to California and to Canada, and was avidly involved with séances, a popular pastime.
The New-York Historical Society

The Life and Work of Susan B. Anthony, including Public Addresses, Her Own Letters and Many From Her Contemporaries During Fifty Years. A Story of the Evolution of the Status of Woman. By Ida Husted Harper. In Two Volumes.
Indianapolis: The Bowen-Merrill Company, 1899, 1898
This set is inscribed twice to James B. Pond, American lecture manager (whose clients also included Charlotte Gilman and Harriet Beecher Stowe), in Rochester, New York, on 30 July 1900.
Vol. I: "Yes indeed, you shall have the pen-tracks in memory of the olden days, with the best wishes for the present & future vouchsafe to you and your good wife from your sincere friend & coworker Susan B. Anthony." Vol. II: "With one entire half of the citizens of this Republic still disfranchised—there is yet plenty of room for heroic souls and their most earnest & combined efforts to bring our

46

government into harmony with its Grand Theory of Equal Rights for All—At least so thinks Your old friend Susan B. Anthony."
Eleanor Elliott

Social reformer and woman suffrage advocate, Anthony was an early supporter of temperance and of the abolition of slavery. She attempted to have the Fourteenth Amendment extended to include women. In 1869 she co-founded the National Woman Suffrage Association, and served as President of the Association from 1892 to 1900. She spent her adult life crisscrossing the country seeking support for woman suffrage through lectures and meetings.

In February 1906, at the age of eighty-six, Susan B. Anthony attended her last woman suffrage convention, and confidently proclaimed: "Failure is impossible." A month later—when her amendment had only been ratified by four states—this indomitable New England-born and Quaker-educated spinster died of heart failure. She had led the suffrage movement for fifty years. While the tangled web of political events and maneuverings that preceded the ultimate ratification of the "Nineteenth" on 26 August 1920 are properly the province of historians, two publications in which Susan Anthony played a guiding role belong in the present exhibition.

Asked by her co-suffragists, after her seventy-fifth birthday celebration in 1895, to prepare her reminiscences for publication, she at first protested that she would "rather make history than write it." Nevertheless, she persuaded the African-American journalist, Ida Husted Harper, whom she had met while campaigning in California, to become her official biographer. Harper obliged, and the result is her extensive *Life and Work of Susan B. Anthony*, to which a third volume was added in 1908, two years after Anthony's death. This put Harper in an excellent position to take over the task of editing the *History of Woman Suffrage*. As she remarks in the preface to volume five, "The writers expected when they began in 1877 to bring out one small volume, perhaps only a large pamphlet." Thousands of pages later, Harper chose the cut-off date 1920, and bemoaned the lack of space for important material.

&ℰ "Those scribbling women" The Bestseller

The years preceding and immediately following the Civil War saw the development of what we now call mass market fiction. While a few women tried their hand at adventure tales and lurid crime melodramas, it was the pious and sentimental stories which sold best, filling the new periodicals specifically aimed at women readers, as well as the nationally circulated newspapers like the *New York Ledger*. They were also marketed in cheap hardcover editions, often with appealing decorative bindings clearly meant for the lady's parlor or bedroom. Some of the writing, religious in tone and romantic in theme, offered spiritual consolation to the many women who had lost children to disease or family members to war. Other books adopted the trappings of the Gothic novel to provide entertainment to middle-class women who, with the economy prospering, had been liberated from the most onerous household chores and thus had time to read for pleasure. The most popular of the tales, like those by Maria Cummins, Elizabeth Stuart Phelps, Emma Southworth, and Susan B. Warner offered fantasy, spiritual consolation, and a reinforcement of the social codes that decreed the superior sensitivity of the female.

The financial rewards of writing a popular book could be considerable. If critical acclaim from their male colleagues escaped these authors, as Hawthorne's oft-quoted derogatory phrase suggests it frequently did, they at least did occasionally achieve economic independence—an alluring prospect indeed. Male relatives, like Harriet Lothrop's father, might disapprove of women publishing books and stories, but, as the biographies of the women represented here suggest, writing remained one of the few ways a respectable women, even one left destitute with many children by a ne'er-do-well spouse, could support herself without sacrificing entirely her social position.

Susan Bogert Warner, "Elizabeth Wetherell"
(1819–1885)

The Wide, Wide World. By Elizabeth Wetherell.
New York: Putnam, 1850. 3 volumes
University of Virginia, Taylor Collection of American Best-Sellers

Rejected by numerous prominent New York publishers before finally being accepted reluctantly by George Putnam, at the insistence of his mother, Warner's *Wide, Wide World*, initially brought out under her pseudonym Elizabeth Wetherell, is reported to be the first book by an American author to have sold a million copies. Although her work was precipitated by dire family financial reversals, Warner demonstrated an inborn knack for storytelling in this semi-autobiographical first novel, which recounts the trials and tribulations of a young, self-willed, and spirited American orphan on her journey to spiritual and—as it turns out—material self-fulfillment. For all its pious sentimentality, however, this best-selling nineteenth-century soap opera remains, as one recent critic has aptly put it, "compulsively readable." Sadly, because of rampant literary piracy, she saw only a small portion of the income she should have reaped from her bestseller.

৪১ Maria Susanna Cummins
(1827–1866)

The Lamplighter. A Tale of Thrilling Interest. With Pictorial Illustrations by F. Gilbert, Esq.
Edition in 26 parts: London: John Cassell, 1854
Robert H. Jackson

The Lamplighter.
New York: William L. Allison, [1890?]
This later edition is from the library of the author Susan Glaspell, with "Susie L. Glaspell" written opposite the first page of text, and was purchased by Albert Berg from the estate of Glaspell's husband, George Cram Cook.
New York Public Library, Berg Collection of English and American Literature

What proper mid-nineteenth-century female reader could resist *The Lamplighter*, a "story of a child lost in infancy, rescued from a cruel woman by an old lamplighter, adopted by a blind woman, and later discovered by her well-to-do father"? The answer is that this early-day soap opera by a neophyte author from Salem, Massachusetts, sold 40,000 copies in the first month, and an additional 60,000 before the year 1854 was over. Published as a serial in England, it was soon translated into Danish, French, German, and Italian. Thoroughly irked by *The Lamplighter*'s popularity, Cummins's contemporary and fellow author Nathaniel Hawthorne, whose *The Scarlet Letter* (1850) sold fewer than 10,000 copies during his lifetime, was moved in 1855 to make his now famous complaint to his publisher: "America is now wholly given over to a d————d mob of scribbling women." Maria, daughter of a Salem judge and the product of Mrs. Sedgwick's School for Young Ladies in Lenox (where she knew that lady's sister-in-law Catharine Sedgwick), wrote three more novels of female bravery, set among the urban ordinary and lowly, before her death, still a spinster, at age thirty-nine.

℘ Sara Payson Willis Parton, "Fanny Fern"

(1811–1872)

Ruth Hall. A Domestic Tale of the Present Time. By Fanny Fern.
New York: Published by Mason Brothers, 1855
Barnard College, Overbury Collection

"Fanny Fern" carte de visite.
New York: William Gould, Jr., 1864.
This mounted photograph of the seated, mournful-looking author
was likely to have been mass-produced for publicity purposes.
Mary C. Schlosser

"No happy woman ever writes," the eponymous heroine of Sara
Parton's novel *Ruth Hall*, tells her daughter, reflecting the harsh
reality that had led the author, as well as her main character, to
submit her stories to the press. Although some others in this exhibition clearly prove her wrong, economic hardship and the need to
escape from the misery of genteel poverty was clearly a motivat-
ing force for many mid-century women writers, who found that
they could write and sell stories and sketches without compromis-
ing their respectability, particularly if they could protect their privacy by the use of pseudonyms.

    Ruth Hall is a critical work for understanding the cultural con-
text of women's writing in mid-century America. Filled with all
of the sentimentality and mawkish religiosity that characterize
the worst of the commercial fiction of the time aimed at the
female market, it nonetheless makes quite clear the emotional
struggle women writers underwent in trying to support them-
selves in a society that placed a high value on privacy and female
domesticity. The central character, a widow (and mother) driven
to write by poverty, is refused a job by her brother, a famous editor, before finally succeeding as a popular columnist for a rival
journal. The book was based on fact: Parton's own brother was

Nathaniel Parker Willis, a popular writer of his day who publicly denegrated his sister's writing and her "unfemininely bitter wrath and spite."

℘ Emma Dorothy Eliza Nevitte Southworth

(1819–1899)

"The Hidden Hand. By Emma D. E. N. Southworth, Author of 'The Bride of the Evening,' 'The Deserted Wife,' etc., etc., etc."
The New York Ledger, Volume XIV, No. 48, 5 February 1859, ff.
The New-York Historical Society

The Hidden Hand. A Play Adapted from Mrs. E. D. E. N. Southworth's Celebrated Novel of the Same Name, by Robert Jones Southworth.
New York: As Printed in the New York Ledger, 1867
Columbia University, Rare Book and Manuscript Library

Advertising poster of T. B. Peterson, Publisher, Philadelphia, late 19th century.
Mrs. Southworth is one of the few women whose portrait appears on her publisher's advertising poster. The engraving is captioned "E. D. E. N. Southworth," the sexually-anonymous nom de plume under which all her novels were published by Peterson.
The Library Company of Philadelphia

"Ghosts, abductions, trapdoors, thieves' dens, deserted houses," to name a few of the rusty *dei ex machinae* of the mid-nineteenth-century sentimental romances, provided the stuff of the popular thrillers by this genteelly born Virginian. Southworth was a young woman, pregnant with her second child, when her husband of four years abandoned her and their farm in Wisconsin. She returned to Washington, D.C., and began publishing stories in the *National Era* in 1847 to earn money. She became by far the most prolific of America's prodigious crop of Gothic novelists: in 1877, T. B. Peterson issued an edition of her novels in forty-two volumes. She was also widely recognized in her day as the most skillful and innovative American practitioner of the genre. Her most popular and famous work, *The Hidden Hand*, first appeared as a serial, and was not published separately until almost 30 years later. Its heroine, abducted at birth from her widowed mother by a villainous uncle, suffers the major injustices from which nineteenth-century women had no legal recourse: principally the right to claim her proper and considerable inheritance which, naturally, the evil uncle covets. While earlier heroines of the sentimental Gothic romance were generally extricated from such dilemmas by a hero who is miraculously lurking in the wings and in the final chapter, Southworth endowed her heroine with sufficient boldness of spirit and courage to be able to extricate herself. This novel takes on even more significance as the first book which the American Library Association banned, allegedly because of its references to cross-dressing.

Sara Jane Clarke Lippincott, "Grace Greenwood"

(1823–1904)

A Forest Tragedy, and Other Tales. By Grace Greenwood.
Boston: Ticknor & Fields, 1856
This copy is inscribed by the author to "Henry E. Hill—With the kind regards of Grace Greenwood."
University of Virginia, C. Waller Barrett Collection

New Life in New Lands: Notes of Travel. By Grace Greenwood.
Brooklyn, NY: D. S. Holmes, 1872
This copy is inscribed by the author to her traveling companion, the young Bostonian Lena Russell Harding.
Caroline F. Schimmel

A great-granddaughter of Jonathan Edwards, Lippincott was one of the "scribbling women" writing at the time of Hawthorne's denunciation. Her rather flowery sketches were in vogue in the early 1850s. Unlike many of her fellow sentimentalists, however, Lippincott in later life branched into political action and public life. Hired to write for *Godey's Lady's Book*, she offended many readers by making her anti-slavery views public, and ended up writing instead for the radical abolitionist newspaper, the *National Era*, speaking out for abolition and women's rights.

The American *and* French Revolutions are the setting for *A Forest Tragedy*, an historical saga of a French lieutenant and his faithful Indian companion. Posted in upstate New York, he disobeys orders and elopes with his true love, a half-French Oneida, daughter of the Sachem. Her own sister, righteously stabs her to death, carrying out the vow of the Oneida women to punish those who, "despising their customs and faith," consort with white men. Soon after, accompanied by the Oneida brave who had also loved the slain maiden, our hero is socializing with Lafayette and Marie Antoinette in Paris, and helping democracy come to France. His friend returns to his tribe after two decades, and writes him: "I am in love with barbarism once more. It is degraded, but it is honest."

Lippincott traveled the Lyceum circuit, lecturing on a variety of subjects, and published in a variety of genres, including travel writing and juveniles. She supported herself by writing through the last decades of her life, after her husband had fled abroad to avoid bankruptcy.

During 1871–1872 Lippincott and three friends traveled from Chicago to the West Coast and back. In her account of the tourist trip, *New Life in New Lands*, she depicts America with sardonic wit and occasional feminist spleen. Passing through Wyoming, she allows that "Cheyenne is not an attractive place, but a brave effort is being made to render it less unattractive." The self-abnegation of the Mormon wives in Utah maddened her. The riding skills of the Ute women at a Denver show astonished her. At Yosemite, with all the side-saddles booked, her party rode astride. "If Nature intended woman to ride horseback at all, she doubtless intended it should be after this fashion, otherwise we should have been a sort of land variety of mermaid."

℘ Augusta Jane Evans Wilson
(1835–1909)

St. Elmo. A Novel.
New York: Carleton, 1867
Barnard College, Overbury Collection

Augusta Evans grew up in the then frontier town of Columbus, Georgia and later spent time in Mobile, Alabama, and San Antonio, Texas—the latter providing the inspiration for her youthful first novel, *Inez, A Tale of the Alamo*, written when she was fifteen although not published until 1855. *Inez* and the author's subsequent efforts could not have prepared her for the sensational reception of *St. Elmo*, her extremely successful tale of the reformation of a notorious rake by the beautiful and devout Edna Earl. *St. Elmo*, like its popular ancestors and later descendants, combines a scarcely hidden sensationalism with pious sentimentality, allowing its readers to experience the titillation of romance while rejoicing in the triumph of virtuous gentility.

Wilson was an anti-suffragist and an active supporter of the Confederacy. Her novels were filled with discussions of theology and science, all calculated to reinforce the ultimate victory of faith over wandering doubt. Her discussions of art, music, and painting gave an air of high-minded seriousness to the books which apparently appealed to an audience eager to clothe its taste for entertainment in the cloak of culture.

℘ Elizabeth Stuart Phelps,

later

Mrs. Herbert D. Ward

(1844–1911)

The Gates Ajar.
Boston: Fields, Osgood & Co., 1869
Barnard College, Overbury Collection

Autograph letter, signed, to "Mrs. Lewes" ("George Eliot" [Mary Ann Evans Cross]), 27 July 1875.
In this astonishing letter, Ward advises the by-then world-famous English author, that as part of her course of literary lectures "for boys and girls," she has a whole course about George Eliot and has been showing the children letters Mrs. Lewes (as the lady preferred to be known) had written her. "[A]nd you can fancy my dismay at going one day to my travelling-bag where I had packed your two letters for safe keeping, to find that my little travelling-flask of brandy had leaked out and ruined them both." She requests Mrs. Lewes rewrite them and post them immediately.
New York Public Library, Berg Collection of English and American Literature

In the years following the Civil War, in which so many fathers, brothers, husbands, and lovers had been killed, *The Gates Ajar* offered to its readers the picture of a real and material heaven, designed specifically to console the bereaved female reader to whom neither the rigidities of Calvinist doctrine nor the abstractions of Emersonian belief appealed. The book sold 80,000 copies when it first appeared, and was repeatedly reprinted both in America and in England where, by the end of the century, nearly 100,000 copies had been sold. The popularity of the novel and its "Gates" sequels proved the viability of religious fiction in the commercial market.

Ward was a religious writer, brought up amidst the theological debates of the Andover Seminary in Massachusetts where her Calvinist father was a professor, and author of a dozen or more children's Sabbath books, but she was also a feminist who spoke out strongly for female independence and made no secret of her belief that the church had failed to engage the intelligence and imagination of her contemporaries. Born Mary Gray Phelps, the twelve-year-old took her mother's name when she died in 1852. A popular author and friend of Annie Fields, the elder Elizabeth had been one of the first to use gritty realism in fiction. Her daughter would utilize the same style in some of the twenty-five novels she wrote before her marriage ended her literary career.

𝔊 Mary Abigail Dodge, "Gail Hamilton"
(1833–1896)

The Battle of the Books, Recorded by an Unknown Writer, for the Use of Authors and Publishers: To the First for Doctrine, to the Second for Reproof, to Both for Correction and for Instruction in Righteousness. Edited and Published by Gail Hamilton.
Cambridge, [MA]: Printed at the Riverside Press, and for Sale by Hurd and Houghton, New York, 1870
Barnard College, Overbury Collection

First Love Is Best, by Gail Hamilton.
Boston: Estes and Lauriate, 1877
Yale University, Beinecke Library

Mary Abigail Dodge, the seventh child of James and Hannah Dodge of Hamilton, Massachusetts, was a precocious reader and essayist, who reportedly "took up advanced geography" at the age of five. Educated at the Ipswich Female Seminary, she taught school in Hartford, Connecticut, where she wrote for the local newspapers under the pseudonym Gail Hamilton. In 1858 she moved to Washington, D.C., to become governess of the children of the abolitionist editor of the *National Era*, Gamaliel Bailey.

A rationalist and a witty writer with a deep interest in politics, she was well-known in her own day as a writer of essays. Her first serious work was printed in the *National Era*, but in the years following 1860, when she moved back to Hamilton to nurse her ailing mother, she published more than a dozen volumes of essays and sketches, including her only novel, *First Love Is Best*. From 1865 to 1867 she was an editor of *Our Young Folks*, a popular juvenile periodical that later merged with *St. Nicholas*.

Distressed by the control of gentlemen publishers over royalties and distribution, Dodge lashed out angrily in *The Battle of the Books*. Her bitter arguments urging equality between writer and publisher gave voice to frustrations particularly felt by women authors. Like other prominent women writers of her generation, Dodge was a staunch foe of woman suffrage. Among her anti-suffrage diatribes were *Woman's Wrongs—A Counter-Irritant* and *Women's Worth and Worthlessness*.

Anna Katharine Green Rohlfs
(1846–1935)

The Leavenworth Case, A Lawyer's Story. By Anna Katharine Green.
New York: G. P. Putnam's Sons, 1878
Columbia University, Rare Book and Manuscript Library

Anna Katharine Green was the author of the first American detective story published by a woman under her own name. Over a million copies *of The Leavenworth Case* were sold. Compared favorably by her contemporaries to Poe and Conan Doyle (whose Sherlock Holmes did not appear until 1887), Green here created Inspector Gryce of the Metropolitan Police. In a series of novels, Gryce was to solve ingenious crimes, often encountering inventive murder weapons—ice bullets, for example.

Green, who married a thespian and became the mother of

three and the family breadwinner, went on to invent two female detectives, first Amelia Butterworth, a Miss Marple-like amateur, then in 1915 Miss Violet Strange, who had the distinction of being the first woman entering into detective work as a professional.

𝓕𝓪 Ann West Adams Fields, "Annie Fields"
(1834–1915)

The Life and Letters of Harriet Beecher Stowe.
Boston & New York: Houghton, Mifflin, 1897
A presentation copy, this volume has an autograph letter dated Christmas 1897 from Annie Fields to Mabel Lowell, the daughter of James Russell Lowell, which refers to her father's kind letter to Stowe about *The Minister's Wooing.*
Mary C. Schlosser

An invitation to a soirée at the Charles Street home in Boston of Mr. and Mrs. James T. Fields meant one was sure to encounter America's literary lions such as Longfellow, Lowell, Whittier, Holmes, and Harriet Beecher Stowe—to name a few of the distinguished writers who frequented Annie Fields' "salon," as it came to be known. The daughter of a prominent Boston physician and his socially impeccable wife, young Annie was projected into the Boston literary world by virtue of her marriage in 1854 to Fields, seventeen years her senior, who was then well on his way to becoming one of Boston's most prominent publishers.

While married to Fields, Annie was able to write and publish two respectable volumes of poetry and an anonymous novel (*Asphodel*, 1866), but her literary fulfillment began after her husband's death in 1881, when she started a series of literary reminiscences in which she combined the charm of her salon days with the memories of the friendships that ensued. Though edited in deference to so-called "good taste" and drawn also from her large correspondence, these volumes are as much a tribute to a famous hostess as they are to the author's subjects. In her later years, she lived with and supported the writer Sarah Orne Jewett, another clue to the social bonds that at least in Boston assured women of a role in the literary world.

Unabashedly American Regional Writing

In the post-Civil War period, as industry boomed and immigrants arrived from ever more disparate homelands, there was a concomitant sense of the fragility of the natural world. Writers like Sarah Orne Jewett and Mary Murfree gained popularity by pointing out the simplicity and majesty of their own still rural communities. The close observation of local populations and customs that characterized the so-called "local color" writing of the period was particularly suited to women, whose financial situation and family ties often limited the scope of their experience. This regional writing helped to create the nation's understanding of itself as a gathering of diverse peoples, often with common needs.

The genre was instantly denigrated by some "sophisticated" readers. In a 1901 work, *The Aristocrats*, author Lady Helen Pole snootily describes an American acquaintance: "He has encouraged, helped to create, as it were, the latter-day distinctive American literature . . . and was one of the first to make fashionable the story of locality and dialect. (I think he ought to be hanged for that.)" The rather modest scale of the short stories and novels of the genre, however, is deceptive. The works reveal the increasing literary sophistication of authors who had learned their skills by avidly reading European masters like de Maupassant, Tolstoy, and Turgénev. They also evinced a growing professionalism, which earned the respect of editors, critics, and colleagues like William Dean Howells and Henry James.

ᏜᎾ Alice Cary

(1820–1871)

Clovernook, or Recollections of Our Neighborhood in the West.
Clinton Hall, NY: Redfield, 1852
Caroline F. Schimmel

Autograph letter to Horace Greeley, New York, 1868.
Cary, though by this time a noted author of several books, shows
herself a master of melodrama. She complains alternately that
she has no friends and that she cannot count on her friends. "I
came to this great City nearly twenty years ago in blind ignorance
of myself and the world, without literary education . . . without
money, without health, without a friend to speak one word for
me. . . ."
The Pierpont Morgan Library, New York (MA 5011)

Born on a farm in rural Hamilton County, Ohio, eight miles
north of Cincinnati, Alice Cary and her younger sister Phoebe
(1824–1871) both became prolific poets whom their friend John
Greenleaf Whittier was later to enthusiastically characterize as
the "sweet singers of the West." Actually, although the poetic
efforts of the two Western sweet singers had a certain popular
impact on readers of the periodicals of the day, it is in her prose
sketches and short stories that Alice Cary did her most distinctive
work.

Published initially in the *National Era*, an abolitionist weekly
edited by a fellow Ohioan, Cary's *Clovernook* established her as
"one of the earliest regional writers to fictionalize what Eastern
magazines would call 'local color.'" The sisters moved to New
York City, where Alice was determined to earn a living by her
writings. In addition to publishing two more novels in the *Clovernook* mode and three other books, Alice, with her sister, ran a
modest literary salon, frequented by the more genteel New York
writers of her day.

৸ᘒ Rebecca Blaine Harding Davis
(1831–1910)

"Life in the Iron-Mills."
Atlantic Monthly, April 1861
Anthologized in:
Atlantic Tales: A Collection of Stories from the Atlantic Monthly.
Boston: Ticknor & Fields, 1866
Mary C. Schlosser; Library Company of Philadelphia

Margret Howth: A Story of To-Day.
Boston: Ticknor & Fields, 1862
Columbia University, Rare Book and Manuscript Library

Autograph letter to Harper's Magazine, May 20, 1878.
Davis, recently returned from a holiday in Appalachia, proposes
an article on that region, "in view of the real feeling which our
people have for good scenery, and the anxiety for cheap summer
places this year." A savvy self-promoter, Davis describes how deli-
ciously empty that area's by-ways are, averring knowledgeably
that those of the Adirondacks are now full.
The Pierpont Morgan Library, Harper Collection, New York (MA 1950)

The publication of Rebecca Harding Davis's first story, "Life in
the Iron-Mills," appearing unsigned in the April 1861 issue of the
Atlantic Monthly, introduced readers to a world hitherto largely
absent from American fiction, the depressed and polluted environ-
ment of the factory town. The raw realism of its writing led readers to the assumption that the author was male. The impact of
the piece was immediate and dramatic, its critique of industrial
America particularly troubling in the devastating emotional cli-
mate of the Civil War.

Harding's next book was also serialized anonymously in the
Atlantic as "A Story of To-Day" and later published as *Margret
Howth.* It contained another bitter indictment of the selfishness
and egotism she saw invading modern life. Her heroine showed
that a willingness to work for others could alleviate one's complic-

ity in the sufferings brought by unrestrained greed. When James T. Fields, editor of the *Atlantic Monthly*, persuaded Davis to give her story a happy ending to bring it into the tradition of sentimental fiction, the power of the book was diminished and the author's role as a precursor of the "naturalist" writers like Frank Norris and Theodore Dreiser was largely obscured. Ironically, despite her moving and popular fiction, she was still best known as the wife of the managing editor of the Philadelphia *Inquirer* and the mother of war correspondent and romantic novelist Richard Harding Davis.

℘ Sarah Orne Jewett
(1849–1909)

Deephaven.
Boston: James R. Osgood, 1877
Barnard College, Overbury Collection

The Country of the Pointed Firs.
Boston: Houghton, Mifflin, 1896
This copy was inscribed by the author to Dr. Charles Hayes.
Iola S. Haverstick

Sarah Orne Jewett's considerable fictional output is anchored in the upriver seaport town of South Berwick, Maine, where she was born, and in the surrounding countryside which she came to know as a young girl when she accompanied her country doctor father on his rounds. For, as she was to explain in later life, "When I was, perhaps fifteen, the first 'city boarders' began to make their appearance near Berwick; and the way they misconstrued the country people and made game of their peculiarities fired me with indignation. I determined to teach the world that country people were not the awkward, ignorant set these persons seemed to think . . . [and] to know [instead] their grand, simple lives; and so far as I had a mission, when I first began to write, I think that was it." Omitted here is Jewett's life-long preoccupation with, and study of, the craft of fiction which was to elevate the ostensibly commonplace matter of her sketches and short stories into the realm of literature. Though the spinster author's life in Berwick was to be punctuated by frequent trips to Europe, as well as by extensive stays in Boston, fittingly Jewett died, a few months shy of her sixtieth birthday, in the same house in which she had been born.

At the urging of William Dean Howells, then editor of the prestigious *Atlantic Monthly*, the magazine in which Jewett had published much of her early fiction, the fledgling author revised, with additions, those of her earlier sketches with a common setting into what one recent critic has aptly denoted as the "loose-leaf novel" format. In the resulting *Deephaven*, Jewett's first published book, two young women from well-to-do city families decide to spend the summer visiting the fishing village of Deephaven, where one of them has ancestral connections. Not only do the visitors come to know and appreciate the "grand, simple lives" of Jewett's rural neighbors, but also, and more significantly, *Deephaven* proved to be the precursor of its author's more skillful stories and sketches still to come.

In *The Country of the Pointed Firs*, Jewett returned to the format she had used twenty years earlier in her initial "loose leaf novel," *Deephaven*. In *Pointed Firs*, however, the author replaced the somewhat snobbish adolescent summer visitors of *Deephaven* with a middle-aged, urban, and urbane woman writer who also serves as the book's narrator. While the thin plot of *Pointed Firs* involves the unnamed narrator's progress from initial outsider to her gradual acceptance as a part of the Dunnet Landing community, what makes the book memorable is Jewett's skillful depiction of her coastal village characters whose eccentricities and seemingly barren lives are counterpointed by the vital beauty of their surroundings. As one critic put it: "By an artful balancing of intensive and contradictory emotions and by the unfailing clarity of her descriptive vision, Sarah Jewett achieved in *The Country of the Pointed Firs* one of the classics of American prose writing."

℘ Constance Fenimore Woolson
(1840–1894)

Anne. A Novel. With Illustrations by C. S. Reinhart.
New York: Harper & Brothers, 1882
Barnard College, Overbury Collection

Rodman the Keeper, Southern Sketches.
New York: D. Appleton & Company, 1886
This copy is from the libraries of Henry James, with his manuscript notes, and of his biographer, the late Grolier Club member, Leon Edel.
University of Virginia, C. Waller Barrett Collection

Apart from her close friendship with Henry James, Constance Fenimore Woolson has largely been ignored by twentieth-century literary historians and critics. Yet during her lifetime, Woolson's novels and short story collections were well received by the contemporary reading public.

Born in New Hampshire, Woolson was the the great-niece of James Fenimore Cooper and the daughter of a stove manufacturer who, during Constance's infancy, moved his family to Cleveland, Ohio. The family summered on Michigan's Mackinac Island, which was to provide the background for Woolson's first novel. Described as a rambling episodic narrative, *Anne* was actually a mystery thriller and would sell over 57,000 copies.

Although Woolson continued to produce her particular brand of fiction for the rest of her life, including the short stories collected in *Rodman the Keeper*, the popularity of her later fiction never came close to the sales and acclaim accorded *Anne*. After years of living with her mother in New England and Florida, when that lady died in 1879, Constance moved to Europe. She became a close friend of Henry James and when, prompted possibly by debt or by her increasing deafness, she jumped from her Venetian apartment window, the suicide prompted James to write to a friend, "She was the gentlest and tenderest of women, and full of intelligence and sympathy."

℘⅁ Mary Noailles Murfree, "Charles Egbert Craddock"
(1850–1922)

In the Tennessee Mountains.
Boston: Houghton, Mifflin, 1884
Caroline F. Schimmel

Mary Murfree came from the prominent West Tennessee family that gave its name to the city of Murfreesboro and that lost everything in the Civil War. Never married, she was a popular and prolific writer, who published more than twenty-five volumes of fiction, mostly short stories. She first broke into print in 1884, when two of her stories, "The Dancin' Party" and "Harrison Cove," were published in the *Atlantic Monthly* and her first novel, *In the Tennessee Mountains*, appeared.

Murfree was a classic regionalist writer whose best stories depicted the rural types that populated the isolated mountain communities of the Great Smokey Mountains, where she had summered since childhood. Despite being lame, even as a child Murfree rode the mountain trails on horseback, absorbing the natural beauties and befriending the scattered settlers eking out an existence there. *In the Tennessee Mountains*, and her next four novels, described the conflict between local beliefs and superstitions on the one hand, and the "modern" social order on the other. With Appalachia then much in the news, as Easterners avidly followed the trials of the reportedly awesomely in-bred and backward Hatfields and McCoys, Murfree tried to provide an antidote, defending the mores of mountain people. Her city-dwelling tourists were always shown as superficial and devoid of common sense, in contrast to her lowly backwoods heroines, who though seemingly ignorant, could call a spade a spade and were infused with "moral splendors."

℘ Mary Eleanor Wilkins Freeman
(1852–1930)

A New England Nun, and Other Stories.
New York: Harper & Brothers, 1891
This copy was inscribed to a Mr. Kendrick by the author in December of 1891.
University of Virginia, C. Waller Barrett Collection

Pembroke.
New York: Harper & Brothers, 1894
Barnard College, Overbury Collection

Two autograph letters to Mary Louise Booth, editor of Harper's Magazine *(and author of a seven-volume* History of the City of New York*), dated 26 January 1887 and 29 June 1888.*
The author, who signs her letters "Pussy Willow," encloses three Christmas stories for publication with the first letter, and a poem and a Thanksgiving tale with the second. In both letters, she is unhappy, almost contrite with her submissions. Booth had been her literary mentor since she turned to writing as an indigent orphan of thirty-one.
New York Public Library, Berg Collection of English and American Literature

Mary Wilkins Freeman is known today primarily as the author of short stories depicting the Calvinists of northern New England as they survived into the industrial age. She was a prolific writer whose success was recognized when she was awarded the William Dean Howells Gold Medal for fiction by the American Academy of Arts and Letters in 1926. In stories such as "A New England Nun," "The Village Singer," and "The Revolt of Mother," Freeman explored the strength and eccentricity of the New England character, in particular the village women whose independence of spirit allowed them to escape the narrow roles that fate seemed to have determined for them. A self-supporting spinster until age forty-nine, Wilkins married a doctor from New Jersey whose alcoholism and other mental problems would preoccupy the author until she legally separated from him in 1919.

In *Pembroke*, her most successful and popular novel, Freeman depicts both the harshness of the Puritan legacy and the human consequences of the moral rigidity it begets. Two men quarrel over politics and blight their own lives, and those of the women around them. A mother beats her son for transgressing God's will and her own, and inadvertently kills him. The details of life in a small community and the glimpses of farming and village life serve to soften the violence of the plot, making the novel one of the most effective examples of local-color writing.

℘ꝺ Celia Laighton Thaxter
(1835–1894)

Autograph letter, signed, Isles of Shoals, 2 June 1883.
Thaxter, while pleased to run a rustic "salon" for the New England art colony and literati, at her hotel and at her home on the island, rarely penned criticism of their work. This long letter is an affectionate, but detailed analysis of some poetry sent by a friend, a private glimpse into the mind of an author.
Caroline F. Schimmel

An Island Garden, with Pictures and Illustrations by Childe Hassam.
Boston & New York: Houghton, Mifflin, 1894
Signed by both Hassam and Daniel Berkeley Updike, the book's designer, this copy also contains a tipped-in letter from Celia Thaxter to the "Dear Eds. Scribner." Writing from Appledore in

November 1873, the fairly neophyte poet "heartily" thanks them
for proofs [from *Scribner's Monthly?*] and returns them duely corrected.

Iola S. Haverstick

One of America's better-known poets during her lifetime, Celia
Thaxter is chiefly remembered today for the meticulous prose classic, *An Island Garden*, her final book, published a few months before her death. She was born in Portsmouth, New Hampshire, the
daughter of Thomas Laighton, a merchant who dabbled in local
politics. In 1839, the family sailed to White Island, the smallest
of the Isles of Shoals, some nine miles off the Portsmouth coast,
where he had been appointed lighthouse keeper. There young Celia
came to know the pleasures and perils of island living which later
were to become the staples of her poetic imagery. Island life continued on Appledore, the largest of the Shoals group where Laighton,
in partership with Levi Thaxter, a young Harvard graduate who
also functioned as tutor to the Laighton children, built Appledore
House. Designed as a summer hotel, it would attract such artistic
luminaries as Emerson, Hawthorne, and Mark Twain, and the
painters Childe Hassam and William Morris Hunt.

When she was barely sixteen, Celia married Thaxter, who
soon became disenchanted with island life and in 1856 moved his
wife and their two young sons to Newtonville, Massachusetts. As
an outlet for her homesickness, Celia began writing poetry about
life on the island, which was published in the major periodicals of
the day and which, in due course, earned her a literary reputation.
Separated from Levi in 1869, Celia Thaxter spent the last twenty-
five summers of her life on her beloved Appledore, where she
helped her two younger brothers run the hotel and cultivated a
summer salon and her equally famous garden. The first edition of
An Island Garden represents a magical collaboration between writer
and painter, each celebrating the beauties of a remarkable landscape. The ornamental design for the cover of the exhibition catalogue is taken from that by Sarah de St. Prix Wyman Whitman
for *An Island Garden*.

On the Edge
Writers from the West

While most nineteenth-century books and periodicals were printed and published in and about the Eastern seacoast cities, from the
time that Mary Rowlandson's captivity narrative first appeared in
1682, the lore of the American frontier and frontier life fascinated
readers in all parts of the world. Stories of the hardships of Western life (however far east that Western border may seem to us
now) had always offered readers the excitement and titillation
of danger, often followed by the satisfactions of redemption and
the restoration of order. When women addressed these themes,
they often included details that were uncommon in the potboilers
of their male contemporaries. Frequently, as in the works of the
transplanted Easterner Caroline Kirkland, they cast a sardonic eye
on their neighbors and the domestic arrangements of frontier life.
At their best, novelists like Helen Hunt Jackson and the less well-
known Mary Hunter Austin combined a respect for the land with
an impassioned clarity about the role of its conquerors, its tradi-
tions, and its new and its old inhabitants. Probably the most popular synthesis of the new, proud patriotism of the period was the
poem written by Wellesley College professor Katharine Lee Bates,
inspired by her 1893 vacation in Colorado. Aptly titled "America
the Beautiful," it opens, "O beautiful for spacious skies."

✗ Abigail Jane Scott Duniway

(1834–1915)

Captain Gray's Company; or, Crossing the Plains and Living in Oregon.
Portland, OR: Printed and Published by S. J. McCormick, 1859

Caroline F. Schimmel

"Jenny" Scott, daughter of a large Kentucky family, emigrated with her parents and many siblings by wagon train to Oregon in 1852. An avid writer, young Jenny kept a detailed journal of the six-month journey, during which her mother died of cholera and she herself became very ill. After marriage and homesteading with a financially inept husband, she decided to use her journal as the basis for a full-length novel. *Captain Gray's Company*, the first commercially published novel printed in Oregon, appeared a month after the birth of her third of six children. Duniway would later become the owner of a printing plant in Portland and the publisher and editor of an influential woman suffrage newspaper, *New Northwest*.

Duniway's book uses dialect to highlight the class division between the Yankee settlers in Illinois and in Oregon, and the supposedly more primitive settlers from elsewhere who surround them. Her heroines clearly represent her support of independent women, one of whom, a young farm wife, urges her female neighbors to enjoy the fresh air and water of Oregon and to resist the pressure to have "more than two [sic] children a year." Contemporary male reviewers complained about the love stories and her depiction of weak, hen-pecked husbands.

✄ Helen Maria Fiske Hunt Jackson
(1830–1885)

Printed contract of Harper & Brothers for A Century of Dishonor, completed in ink, signed "Helen Jackson" and dated 21 May 1880.
Harper offered Jackson $250 for the completed work, against 10% of sales. She requested copies of the book rather than cash. Complaining to friends that the contract was overly complicated, she would return to Roberts Brothers, her usual publisher, for the second edition in 1885, with a new introduction by her traveling companion, Sarah Woolsey.
Columbia University, Rare Book and Manuscript Library

A Century of Dishonor.
New York: Harper & Brothers, 1881
Caroline F. Schimmel

Autograph letter, signed, to Mary Louise Booth, editor of Harper's Magazine, 26 January 1884.
In this window on the publishing world, Jackson and her editor (and friend) at the magazine disagree about exactly how much her work is worth. The ire is barely veiled as Jackson dissembles: "Of course neither you nor I 'haggle'! Your stating your views & my stating mine, is not haggling—only simple business. Nobody can be better aware than I am that literary work is not paid according to 'equal merit' . . . It is a great while since I have been paid by the page, or by counted words. And a still longer time since I have received so small a sum as $10 for any poem. . . ."
Caroline F. Schimmel

Ramona.
Boston: Roberts Brothers, 1884
Caroline F. Schimmel

Though the daughter of a socially prominent Amherst College professor of languages, Jackson had an erratic education, especially after the death of both parents while she was still in her teens.

Marriage in 1852 to Edward Hunt, a brilliant physicist and brother of the governor of New York, brought her a few years of happiness and two children. The death of both her sons and then her husband's 1865 demise in a submarine he was inventing, impelled the casual poet to a full-time literary career.

Jackson's prolific though largely undistinguished writings earned her sufficient money to enable her to travel, visiting friends in the Western states and in Europe. On one visit to Colorado in 1876, she met and married a local banker, a Quaker from Pennsylvania. Unable to live happily in such a remote setting, despite a constant flow of guests from the East, Jackson spent most of her later years traveling and accumulating the details that made possible the publication of the two works for which she is best known.

Jackson was already a popular writer of poetry, travel narratives, and children's books, when she and the author Sarah Woolsey ("Susan Coolidge") first toured the West in 1872. When, in Boston in 1879, she heard the chief of the Oklahoman Ponca tribe describe the theft of that tribe's gold-rich land by the United States and the forced removal of his people, she was converted to the Indian cause. She would use her writing and merchandising skills to rail against the misery and miserliness she saw in the conduct of the Bureau of Indian Affairs.

The result of her nascent political efforts, A Century of Dishonor, was a scholarly and systematic study, published in 1881, with a quotation from Benjamin Franklin on its crimson covers: "Look upon your hands! They are stained with the blood of your relations." She sent the book at her own expense to members of Congress, but it was uniformly ignored by officialdom—Theodore Roosevelt later called it "thoroughly untrustworthy."

Deliberately styled after Harriet Beecher Stowe's Uncle Tom's Cabin, Jackson's Ramona is a full-blown romance about the then-tottering Spanish society of California and the Mission Indians whose lands were being usurped. Although it did not have the international impact of Mrs. Stowe's book, the novel was instantly popular, selling 7,000 copies in the first three months after it was printed. It continued to attract readers throughout the twentieth century, and was produced in at least three hundred more printings, three movie versions, and a number of plays. Although *Ramona* did little to change government ways, the book prompted a steady stream of readers to visit California, looking for the places mentioned, and thus spurred the nascent tourist industry of the Southwest. Helen Hunt Jackson died of cancer the year after the publication of her novel, her crusade scarcely begun.

Sarah Winnemucca,
later
Mrs. Lewis Hopkins
(1844–1891)

Life Among the Paiutes: Their Wrongs and Claims, Edited by Mrs. Horace Mann.
Boston: Cupples, Upham & Co.; New York: G. P. Putnam's Sons, 1883
Caroline F. Schimmel

A daughter and granddaughter of Paiute leaders who felt their tribe could only survive by learning the ways of their occupiers, Thocmetony (Shell Flower) was renamed Sarah and sent to a seminary in San Jose, California. Although later expelled because of complaints of white parents, Sarah learned enough English (she was fluent in three Indian languages) to become a prized army liaison in Nevada and Oregon. Even her great diplomatic skills, however, were insufficient to stop the remnants of her peaceful tribe from being forced to the Yakima Reservation near Fort Vancouver, Washington, when Secretary of the Interior Carl Schurz reneged on his 1879 promise to her. Helen Hunt Jackson, another opponent of Schurz, used an 1870 essay by Winnemucca documenting government corruption in her *Century of Dishonor* in

1881. In 1883 Sarah and her second husband, Lewis Hopkins, jour-
neyed again to the East Coast, where her popular lecture series
again had no impact on Washington, D.C. She turned to her Boston
friend Mary Mann for help in writing and publicizing her story.

Life Among the Paiutes, the first popularly published work by an
American Indian, is both a personal reminiscence and a bitter complaint against the United States for its treatment of the Paiute tribe.
Its descriptions provided the general public of the late nineteenth
century with a vivid, sympathetic picture of an otherwise invisible
subculture.

ℱ Gertrude Horn Atherton
(1857–1948)

Los Cerritos.
New York: John W. Lovell Company, 1890
An early owner has pasted a portrait of the author, clipped from a
periodical, opposite the title.
Caroline F. Schimmel

Erratically educated, a child of divorce raised on a California ranch,
at age seventeen Gertrude eloped with a half-Chilean who had been
courting her mother. Undomesticated, despite having a husband
and two children, bored, and grumpy, she wrote a thinly disguised
piece on a local scandal for the San Francisco *Argonaut* in 1883 which
made her even less welcome in that city. Fortunately (for her ambitious self) her husband died in 1887 in a shipwreck, and she abandoned her children and departed for her perceived Elysian Fields—
New York and Europe. There this ambitious, pretentious young
woman spoke with disdain of American (i.e., "bourgeois") writing, pooh-poohing the efforts of Walt Whitman, William Dean
Howells, and Ella Wheeler Wilcox. Ironically, she would soon
return to her "roots," setting nearly half of her writing in contemporary and historic California.

Los Cerritos, her maiden effort, resembles Sally Wood's *Julia and the Illuminated Baron*, written nearly a century before. Awash with throbbing emotions and plot twists, both tales interweave fiction with factual characters in an exotic (to Eastern readers) setting. Atherton's dewy-eyed, yet instinctively savvy heroine is the child of the outlaw Joachim Murietta. Raised amongst the wretched Hispanic squatters of a California valley ranch, Carmelita and the local padre enlighten the uncaring, incredibly rich landowner who has forcibly evicted the settlers. He pays attention to the padre's lecture on Henry George because, embarrassingly for him, Carmelita saved his life when he was assaulted by a squatter leader. What would later set Atherton apart from, and above, local colorists was both her unique, extensive research into Spanish-ruled California and her fascination with the relationships between men and women.

℘ Ina Donna Coolbrith
(1842–1928)

Songs of the Golden Gate.
Boston & New York: Houghton, Mifflin, 1895
This copy is inscribed to John Howell, the eminent San Francisco rare book dealer.
Caroline F. Schimmel

Born Josephine D. Smith, she was nine when her mother, step-father, and siblings moved to Los Angeles. By age eleven, she was being published in the local newspaper. Married and divorced by the time she was forty, she moved to San Francisco, invented the persona of "Ina Donna Coolbrith," and began writing full time. Befriended by Bret Harte, Ambrose Bierce, and Mark Twain, she soon gained a literary reputation of her own as a "lady poet," publishing in most of the national periodicals. The majority of her works are focused on nature and the family, suitable topics for women at that time, but the results are infused with a spontaneity and perceptivity that few poets achieve. In 1915 she was named the first Poet Laureate of California.

Songs of the Golden Gate was her third and final collection of poetry. Though quite popular in her day, Coolbrith has yet to be rediscovered. In fact, a large portion of the Book Club of California's anthology of her poetry, *California*, beautifully printed by John Henry Nash in 1918 in an edition of 500, was still sitting in the Club's offices forty years later, where it was destroyed by a flood.

℘ Mary Hunter Austin
(1868–1934)

The Land of Little Rain.
Boston & New York: Houghton, Mifflin, 1903
Caroline F. Schimmel

Typed letter with manuscript postscript to Alice Corbin, signed "M. A.," written about 1917.
Corbin, her long-time friend and fellow member of the "literati" of New Mexico, has just sent to her Amy Lowell's new book, *Men, Women and Ghosts*. Austin is astonished and inspired and yet critical of the introduction's apologetic tone: "it is pitiful" that Lowell not recognize that she is "setting forth boldly on that adventure to take the poetic measure of a child's hoop and a shuttlecock!"
Caroline F. Schimmel

When Mary Austin's only child was born profoundly retarded, she blamed her husband's faulty ancestry, but her mother blamed her. The conflict resulted in her having two nervous breakdowns, and it was on the advice of a psychiatrist in San Francisco that she determined on a writing career.

From her first published story, "The Mother of Felipe," appearing in *The Overland Monthly* in 1892, Austin carved a niche for herself in American literature. Obsessed with place, her talent lay in depicting the specialness of the American desert landscape and its original inhabitants. Although she was happiest as the doyenne of salons in Carmel and Santa Fe and wrote her magisterial autobiography in the third person, her descriptive prose shines with the grace and awe of nature. The settings of her works are, she said, where "life stood at the breathing pause between the old ways and the new."

The Land of Little Rain was Austin's first published book, a set of fourteen essays describing Mohave Desert locations near Inyo and Bishop. Although Austin's mother, a fan of Lydia Maria Child and Maria Cummins, cruelly told her that the stories were "beyond me," the volume sold well, and was followed by thirty more books and innumerable articles in magazines and newspapers.

Bertha Muzzy Sinclair,
later
Bertha M. Cowan; "B. M. Bower"
(1871–1940)

Chip of the Flying U.
New York: G. W. Dillingham, 1906
Caroline F. Schimmel

Few biographical facts are known about this once popular writer, who has lately become a cult figure among collectors of Western Americana. Raised on a Montana ranch, she was married three times, had three children with her second husband, and lived in at least five western states. Her books—the first by a woman in the Western pulp genre—were generally published under the male-sounding pseudonym of B. M. Bower or as B. M. Sinclair. As late as 1936, a new work's dust jacket referred to the author as "he."

Muzzy's first novel, *Chip of the Flying U*, was set in Montana and featured a hero who was the prototype of all her heroes—tall, handsome, sensitive, quiet, yearning to be an artist. Her women are more colorful, sometimes being doctors or ranch managers. Her plots were often hackneyed, but the details of ranch life were accurate, vivid, and even humorous. Her collaboration with painter and illustrator Charles M. Russell, said to be the model for Chip, helped her books to become bestsellers.

The eager public received sixty-six more novels and anthologies, all of which used western settings in which Muzzy had lived. Titles such as *The Happy Family*, *The Range Dwellers*, and *Cabin Fever*, along with *Chip of the Flying U*, helped keep the myth of the romantic and adventure-filled West alive for several generations of readers.

℘ American Girls
The Juvenile Market

Writing for children, although not exclusively a feminine preroga-
tive, always fell within the domestic sphere ascribed to women by
tradition and logic. Throughout the eighteenth and nineteenth
centuries, the writing of Sunday School texts and moral tales for
youngsters was both a highly respectable and lucrative occupation
for female writers. Then, in the middle of the century, educators
like Elizabeth Peabody and Catharine Beecher, who propounded
girls' literacy through private and public schools, also prepared the
way for the entrance of women into the teaching profession. After
the Civil War, a new generation, more secular in outlook and
background, had a new vision of the American child. The books
written by women to entertain and instruct these children depict
young people, often girls on the verge of adolescence, who have
more independence and less supervision than their contemporaries abroad. Rich in detail and sensibility, the novels stand as
American contributions to the golden age of children's literature.

These works still appeal to audiences in a way that adult novels of the period seldom do. They are fresh and often funny. The
issues such juvenile tales touch on—in particular the difficulties
of reconciling personal independence with family life—have
remained alive. The children's tales also awaken a yearning for a
close, happy family life that seemed as idyllic to readers then as to
those today. Some authors cleverly, and perhaps unconsciously,
combined the psychological and scenic realism of the regional fiction of the period with what might be called "domestic romance."
Many other perennial favorites, including *Daddy Long Legs*, *A Girl
of the Limber-lost*, and the Canadian *Anne of Green Gables*, are only
omitted for lack of space in the exhibition. They are never out of
print and have frequently been adapted for the screen.

𝓕𝔞 Mary Elizabeth Mapes Dodge
(1830–1905)

Hans Brinker; or, The Silver Skates. A Story of Life in Holland.
New York: James O'Kane, 1865
This copy was inscribed by the author, "For Annie With love and best wishes of her friend Mary E. Dodge May 31st 66."
University of Virginia, C. Waller Barrett Collection

St. Nicholas, Vol. 1, No. 1.
New York, 1872
Columbia University, Rare Book and Manuscript Library

Autograph letter, 4 pages, to Elsie Lyde, daughter of a New York friend, from "my box at the Cordova," c. December 1888
In this enchanting missive to the seven-year-old actress (known professionally as Elsie Leslie), then starring in *Little Lord Fauntleroy* on Broadway, Dodge pretends to be her own "dear little dog Fido," writing to the little girl's doll: " . . . my paws are pretty stiff so you must excuse my poor penmanship. . . . There is no Harvard Annex for dogs. . . . I forgot to say I have to be wound up with a key. Do you? Does mamma have to be wound up before she plays Lord Fauntleroy?"
The Pierpont Morgan Library, New York (MA 3897)

Widowed with two children at the age of twenty-seven, Mary Mapes Dodge worked with her father on the publication of several New Jersey periodicals before writing the novel for children for which she is best remembered today, *Hans Brinker*. The lasting popularity of this story of frozen canals and skating races has generally overshadowed Dodge's even more impressive accomplishment, the founding and administration of America's most widely-read children's magazine, *St. Nicholas*, which published continuously until 1905.

A gifted and imaginative editor who was responsible almost singlehandedly for shaping what has often been known as the

Golden Age of children's literature, Dodge, whose judgment and sense of the market was widely respected, corresponded with almost all of the well-known authors of her day. Though the magazine seldom escaped the social stereotyping and middle-class values that its audience embraced, Dodge was a thoughtful negotiator between the moral uprightness demanded by the adult establishment and the simpler, more imaginative realism enjoyed by children.

℘ Louisa May Alcott
(1832–1888)

Little Women, or, Meg, Jo, Beth and Amy. Illustrated by May [i.e., Amy] Alcott.
Boston: Roberts Brothers, 1868–1869. 2 volumes
New York Public Library, Berg Collection of English and American Literature

Work: A Story of Experience.
Boston: Roberts Brothers, 1873
Barnard College, Overbury Collection

"Most women do whatever they can." Autograph manuscript, 1884.
The title sums up this poignent four-line poem on woman's lot, and indeed the exhibition.
New York Public Library, Berg Collection of English and American Literature

As the daughter of the high-minded, albeit invariably impoverished, Transcendentalist philosopher and educator, Bronson Alcott, Louisa May Alcott's career as an author centered on her compulsive and continuing struggle to liberate her family from the stigma of poverty—and occasional ridicule—brought about by her father's impractical schemes. That she eventually succeeded in achieving her ambition is a tribute both to her innate skill as writer and storyteller and to her ever-present willingness to accommodate this skill to the popular demands of an increasingly urban public. Worn out by her frantic exertions—some 270 published works, including, apart from her famous juveniles, several so-called "adult" novels, and a spate of short stories and other miscellaneous items—and beset by various nervous disorders, she died at age fifty-four on the day of her father's funeral.

Later described by its author as "the golden egg" that rescued her family from poverty, Alcott's most celebrated juvenile was originally published in two parts. The illustrations were drawn by her sister Amy (who used an anagram for her name on the title page). Scarcely had the first part of Little Women appeared in September 1868 than Alcott's publishers were besieged by some 4,000 orders for the second part, duly published in April 1869. By the close of the year, readers had already gobbled up 3,800 copies of Alcott's "golden egg." While the appeal of Little Women, a semi-autobiographical tale of the trials, tribulations, and triumphs of the March sisters, has been described as defining "once and for all the values of the American middle-class home of the period," from a literary perspective, Alcott's seemingly unvarnished depictions of everyday realities in this and her subsequent works pioneered a new direction in American juvenile fiction.

Following the overwhelming success of Little Women, Alcott found herself deluged by incessant demands from editors and publishers for her writing, which, for the most part, she obliged at a pace that was ultimately to lead to her undoing. To a request from Henry Ward Beecher's Christian Union for a serial, however, she wisely (for once) responded by "dusting off," as one biographer has termed it, an earlier unpublished novel begun some five years before Little Women. Originally entitled Success, Work is Alcott's second adult—and most autobiographical—fiction. It is a recapitulation of its author's earlier experiences as a domestic servant in various households in the affluent Boston suburb of Dedham. To the extent that Work realistically portrayed the economic plight that young American women like Alcott, caught without vocation or training, frequently faced in a rapidly developing urban industrial society, the novel lives up to the promise of its original title.

Sarah Chauncey Woolsey, "Susan Coolidge"

(1835–1905)

What Katy Did. A Story. By Susan Coolidge. With Illustrations by Addie Ledyard.
Boston: Roberts Brothers, 1873
Columbia University, Rare Book and Manuscript Library

Sarah Chauncey Woolsey's distinguished ancestors included Timothy Dwight Woolsey, the President of Yale, as well as Jonathan Edwards and Timothy Dwight. She herself maintained a career as a "serious" writer under her own name, saving the pseudonym Susan Coolidge for her immensely more popular children's books. A close friend of Helen Hunt Jackson, with whom she traveled around the American West, she carried on an active career as a writer and as a reader and adviser to the popular Boston publishing firm, Roberts Brothers.

The "Katy" books, perhaps better known in England even today than in America, present the familiar, quasi-autobiographical story of the independent, tomboyish young girl. In *What Katy Did*, the heroine—like Jill in Louisa May Alcott's *Jack and Jill*—injures herself after a daredevil act of disobedience (in this case, a fall from a swing) and painfully learns to control her selfish impulses and conform to the feminine demands of service and obedience during a long period of paralysis and bed rest. Because of Woolsey's gift for the creation of character, the five books in the Katy saga are much more fun than the plot lines lead one to expect. They contain just enough acerbity and rebellious energy to counteract the overt sentimental message.

℔ Lucretia Peabody Hale

(1820–1900)

The Peterkin Papers. With Illustrations.
Boston: James R. Osgood & Co., 1880
The author's name is misspelled on the cover as Lucretia P. Male.
Caroline F. Schimmel

Like so many nineteenth-century American authors, male and
female, Lucretia Hale was the child of a newspaper man. As children, while attending Elizabeth Peabody's school, she and her
seven brothers and sisters (including Edward Everett Hale) printed two morning papers for family consumption, so it was perhaps
not unexpected that, as an unmarried adult, she would help to edit
her brothers' periodicals and write stories herself. A few tales were
published in the *Atlantic Monthly* and *Our Young Folks*, the magazine for children owned by Osgood and Fields who also owned the
Atlantic, but it was the publication of the first of the stories about
the Peterkin family in *Our Young Folks* in 1868 that really began her
literary career.

    The Peterkin Papers and its sequel, *The Last of the Peterkins*,
recount the attempts of a large, not overly-acute family to solve
the problems of everyday life. In a typical tale, the family gets
itself into a hopeless muddle over some ordinary problem, such as
too-sweet tea, and can only be rescued by the timely appearance of
the sensible Lady from Philadelphia who offers an easy solution to
the frantic Peterkins—throw out the tea (to which the family had
by now added salt). Poking fun at the closeness and internal inter-
action of the large Victorian family, the Peterkin stories follow a
comic formula that combines traditional New England values
with a good deal of nonsense. They have remained appealing and
fresh for well over a century.

✍ Harriet Mulford Stone Lothrop, "Margaret Sidney"

(1844–1924)

Five Little Peppers and How They Grew, by Margaret Sidney.
Boston: D. Lothrop and Company, 1880

Caroline F. Schimmel

The child of a prominent church architect and Yale professor, Harriet Stone enjoyed a comfortable middle-class upbringing in New Haven, where she read widely in her father's library. She did not begin publishing fiction until she was in her late twenties, using a pen-name in order to placate her father, who disapproved of women writing for publication. One of her early submissions to the juvenile publication *Wide Awake*, a serial story depicting the adventures of a lively family, the Peppers, evolved into the popular *Five Little Peppers and How They Grew*. The success of the novel, more than 2,000,000 copies of which had been sold before her death, was followed by a dozen sequels about the adventures of the Peppers, as well as numerous other children's stories which have not proven to have the lasting power of her first book.

Harriet Stone's talents attracted the interest of publisher Daniel Lothrop, whom she married in 1881. Her books after that year were published by his juvenile and religious book publishing company, which reportedly survived through her continuing sales. In 1883, the Lothrops bought and restored the house in Concord, Massachusetts, that had been the home of Nathaniel Hawthorne, and before him, of the Alcott family. When her husband died in 1890, she briefly took over the management of his publishing firm. In 1902 Lothrop would save Orchard House, Louisa May Alcott's home, from destruction.

Five Little Peppers concentrates on the homely efforts of a widowed mother and her children to survive such family crises as dead pets, burnt cakes, lost children, and—more seriously—severe illness. In a scenario that must have been familiar to many in the period, the family worries over daily affairs in the little brown house that shelters them, and works hard to make ends meet: eleven-year-old David chops wood for extra money, while the responsible ten-year-old Polly does household chores and keeps an eye on her three irrepressible younger siblings. Mother, the cheerful and saintly Mary Pepper, is the heart of the house, always sympathetic to the troubles of the children, but usually exhausted by hard work. The plot turns on the children's friendship with a wealthy family of young boys, whose long-absent father turns out at the end to be a cousin of the impoverished Mrs. Pepper. Despite its didactic air, the book and its sequels have retained their appeal for the twentieth-century reader because of the author's energetic writing, imbued with a charming sense of the real concerns of childhood.

℘ᴐ Frances Hodgson Burnett
(1849–1924)

Little Lord Fauntleroy.
New York: Charles Scribner's Sons, 1886
First issue. A gift card is laid in this copy, inscribed "Yours sincerely Frances Hodgson Burnett. Washington, D.C."
Barnard College, Overbury Collection

Little Lord Fauntleroy.
New York: Charles Scribner's Sons, 1886
Second issue. This copy was inscribed by the author with a line from the book: "It is a very little thing, perhaps, but it is the best thing of all . . . [to be] born a king." Yours affectionately, Frances Hodgson Burnett.
New York Public Library, Berg Collection of English and American Literature

The Secret Garden.
New York: Frederick A. Stokes, 1911
Yale University, Beinecke Library, Shirley Collection

A prolific writer, Frances Hodgson Burnett made her debut as a writer of adult romances with *That Lass o' Lowries* in 1877. Her first great success, however, was the children's adventure, *Little Lord Fauntleroy*. The appeal of this novel, like that of the even more widely read later books, *The Secret Garden* and *A Little Princess*, lies in its adaptation of already popular American themes to a juvenile audience: the experience of living abroad, the fulfillment of fantasy, and the loneliness of the orphaned or displaced child. Within two years it would also begin a second, equally popular life as a stage play in New York, Boston, London, and Nottingham.

Burnett, called "Fluffy" by her friends, was a flamboyant and not always well-liked character. After Fauntleroy curls and Fauntleroy suits caught on with the American public, she relished her popularity and commercial success. Apart from her novels, her important contribution to the literary profession resulted from her courageous and successful struggle against unauthorized stage adaptations of her fiction. Her victory over a pirated version of *Fauntleroy* had a lasting impact on the struggle for international copyright and earned her the real gratitude of the entire literary establishment.

✦ "The precious words" Verse

Emily Dickinson stands alone in the history of American literature. Her eccentric verse forms and rhythms echo those of Emerson and her use of domestic imagery recalls the metaphysical conceits of Anne Bradstreet, but her voice is unique. Despite her often very local subject matter and vocabulary, which might relegate her to the category of regionalist author, she in fact belongs to no one tradition and she created no school of imitators or followers.

The other poets represented here fall into two very distinct categories. Some, including Celia Thaxter and (early) Harriet Monroe, followed the so-called genteel tradition, writing more or less effective conventional verse in familiar modes. In the early twentieth century, others, like the Imagists Amy Lowell and Hilda Doolittle, searching for a new, fresh poetic mode, broke with tradition. Their work in the years surrounding the first World War cleared the way for the appearance of the even more influential writers to follow. However eager they were to rebel against it and however different in kind and quality their achievements were to be, later writers like Elizabeth Bishop, Louise Bogan, Edna St. Vincent Millay, and Marianne Moore would be the inheritors of a well-established American female poetic tradition.

✦ Emma Lazarus
(1849–1887)

Songs of a Semite.
New York: Office of "The American Hebrew," 1882
The Library Company of Philadelphia

"Success." Autograph manuscript poem, undated.
A typically earnest, even angry work, "Success" opens with the
dark lines, "Oft have I brooded on defeat and pain. / The pathos
of the stupid, stumbling throng." It was published in *The Poems of
Emma Lazarus*.
The Pierpont Morgan Library, New York, (MA 3372)

The Poems of Emma Lazarus.
Boston & New York: Houghton, Mifflin, 1889 [i.e., 1888]
Barnard College, Overbury Collection

Emma Lazarus, the child of a wealthy Sephardic Jewish family in
New York, was educated at home in classics and languages. Her
first book of poems, privately printed in 1866, when she was seventeen, attracted the attention of Emerson, who invited her to
Concord. Like Browning in later years, Emerson became a friend
and an inspiration, and Lazarus dedicated her second volume of
poems to him.

An article she read in the *Century Magazine* in 1882, defending
the pogroms in Czarist Russia, aroused her to the cause that would
occupy her the rest of her short life. She became a student of
Jewish history and turned her energies toward the development of
relief programs for Jewish émigrés. She also translated medieval
Jewish authors and the poems of Heinrich Heine.

Lazarus's most admired work in her own day was her 1882
drama about the fate of twelfth-century Thuringian Jews, "The
Dance to the Death," which is included in *Songs of a Semite*. She is
most famous today as the author of "The New Colossus," a poem
written in 1883 and first published in her 1888 anthology. From it
were taken the lines inscribed on the pedestal of the Statue of
Liberty: "Give me your tired, your poor / Your huddled masses
yearning to be free. . . . "

ᏽᎧ Emily Dickinson

(1830–1886)

Poems of Emily Dickinson, edited by M. L. Todd and T. W. Higginson.
Boston: Roberts Brothers, 1890
Barnard College, Overbury Collection

Poems of Emily Dickinson, Second Series, edited by M. L. Todd and T. W. Higginson.
Boston: Roberts Brothers, 1891
Barnard College, Overbury Collection

Poems of Emily Dickinson, Third Series, edited by M. L. Todd.
Boston: Roberts Brothers, 1896.
This copy comes from the collection of the late, eminent American literature collector, bibliographer, and Grolier Club member Carroll Wilson.
Barnard College, Overbury Collection

"There is no Frigate like a Book / To take us Lands away / Nor any Coursers like a Page / Of prancing Poetry." Born into a distinguished New England family—her grandfather founded Amherst College, her father was a lawyer, judge, and congressman—Emily grew up in Amherst, the shy, sensitive daughter of formal and remote parents. Her best friends were her brother and sister, and other than a year at Mount Holyoke Seminary (later, College) in 1847–1848, her entire life was lived quietly at home. Indeed by the time she was thirty, she had become almost a complete recluse, spending her time reading, corresponding with a few friends, among them Helen Hunt Jackson, and writing poetry. Dickinson was known to have had intense intellectual relationships with several men. One was Benjamin F. Newton who unexpectedly died young. Another was the Rev. Charles Wadsworth, a married man who moved to San Francisco in 1862, just about the time Dickinson withdrew from society. Coincidentally, this was when she became acquainted with Thomas Wentworth Higginson, a poetry critic for the *Atlantic Monthly* (and author of the 1894 biography, *Margaret Fuller d' Ossoli*), with whom she corresponded for over twenty years, but who apparently never urged her to publish her poems.

At her death, hundreds of poems were found in her room, only seven of which had ever been published. Family and friends undertook to publish a selection of her poems which appeared in a series of three books beginning in 1890, the first two volumes being co-edited by Higginson and Mabel Loomis Todd. Additional unpublished material, including her letters, continued to appear in various volumes until as recently as 1961. Her poems are brief intense lyrics of observations on nature, her own life, love, death, denial, and renunciation. Her religious attitudes, the influence of her Puritan heritage, are reflected in the simple hymn-book-like patterns of her verse. But in a few words, her sharp imagistic perception can suggest deep meanings through unexpected turns and striking phrases.

Dickinson, the central figure of many modern novels and tales, also inspired her contemporaries and the writers of the next generation. She is considered the prototype for the heroine of Helen Hunt Jackson's *Mercy Philbrick's Choice* (1876) as well as for Alison Stanhope in Susan Glaspell's *Alison's House* (1930).

৪৯ Harriet Monroe
(1860–1936)

Poetry: A Magazine of Verse.
Chicago: [Published by Harriet Monroe], October, 1912, Volume I, Number 1.
Columbia Unversity, Rare Book and Manuscript Library

Harriet Monroe began her literary career with the private publication of a verse play, *Valerian*, and continued it with the publication of "The Columbian Ode," written to be recited at the opening of the 1892 World Columbian Exposition in Chicago, where she had been appointed poet laureate in response to her insistence that the art of poetry had been overlooked in the celebration. Her importance in American letters, however, stems from her decision in 1910 to publish a periodical to give new poets a public audience. It was to be a monthly review which would, in the words of the initial circular, "give the poets a chance to be heard."

Monroe's instincts were sound. Thanks to her energies and endless editorial work, *Poetry* was a success from the moment it appeared. Between 1912 and 1922, it published, often for the first time in the United States, poetry by H. D., T. S. Eliot, Robert Frost, Amy Lowell, Marianne Moore, Ezra Pound, Carl Sandburg, Wallace Stevens, Sara Teasdale, William Carlos Williams, William Butler Yeats, and many others. If not a brilliant poet, she was an astute editor whose belief in a renaissance of poetry in the opening years of the twentieth century supported and sustained myriad new voices.

᠀ Amy Lowell
(1874–1925)

Men, Women and Ghosts.
New York: Macmillan Company, 1916
This copy was inscribed by the author to Hilda Doolittle ("H. D.") and her husband, Richard Aldington.
University of Virginia, C. Waller Barrett Collection

Amy Lowell's fame as a poet largely rests on the rather melodramatic poetic monologue, "Patterns," that appeared in this, her third collection of verse. Her important role in the development of the modernist movement, however, grew from her good luck and good sense in identifying herself with *Poetry* and the *Little Review* at the moment when new voices in poetry were much in demand. An Imagist Poet, who was later called by Ezra Pound an

"Amygist," Lowell brought to the new poetry a highly-developed taste for publicity, great personal eccentricity, and the cachet of an old, established Boston name. Her public lectures on poetry and drama and her famous Brookline salon, as well as her penchant for smoking cigars, were helpful in establishing the reputations of those contemporaries she admired. *Tendencies in American Poetry* (1917), for example, defended and explained modernism, seeing in such poets as H. D., Robert Frost, Edgar Lee Masters, and Edward Arlington Robinson, the voice of the future.

Hilda Doolittle, "H. D."
(1886–1961)

Sea Garden.
London: Constable and Company, 1916
Columbia University, Rare Book and Manuscript Library

H. D., as Hilda Doolittle was commonly known, is best remembered today as an Imagist Poet and as the troubled bisexual analyzed by Freud. Contemporary and friend of Harriet Monroe, Amy Lowell, William Carlos Williams, and (twice fiancé) Ezra Pound, she married English poet Richard Aldington in 1913, but her nearly fifty-year relationship with the heiress and novelist Bryher (Annie Winifred Ellerman) would outlast marriages and affairs on both sides. A devoted classicist whose subjects reflect a lifelong interest in Greek poetry, myth, and drama, H. D. benefitted from Pound's embrace of the new poets who shared his outlook on the nature and technique of modern verse. She also wrote fiction, autobiography, and dramatic monologues in verse and was for two years literary editor of *The Egoist*.

Sea Garden, H. D.'s first book, contains twenty-seven poems. Short, lyrical, and filled with the concrete, precise delineation of emotion through dense and concentrated imagery, H. D.'s early work has proven to be her most memorable and distinctive.

ℬ The Turn of the Century Transitions

The increasing visibility of women in public life in the last decades of the nineteenth century, fueled by the growth of personal wealth and access to higher education, was matched by a growth in the ambition and scope of writings by women. The publication of Susan B. Anthony's *History of Woman Suffrage* in the late 1880s came at a time when women had already begun to move with confidence into administrative and academic positions, even in the sciences. Women were no longer hesitant to take on political or social issues. Like their male counterparts, they used their writing skills to expose the shortcomings and hypocrisies of modern life. African-American lecturers and educators became more widely seen and read, publicly addressing problems of the post-Reconstruction attitudes toward race, and now also writing popular fiction in an attempt to counteract the romanticism of the hugely popular works of pro-Southern novelists. Female journalist Ida Tarbell took on the mores of American business in "The History of Standard Oil" (*McClure's*, 1902). Travelers "Nellie Bly" [Elizabeth Cochran Seaman] of *The New York World* and Miriam (Mrs. Frank) Leslie astounded the nation with their tales of physical derring-do.

Similar intrepidness is seen in the works of Kate Chopin, who delved courageously into themes seldom mentioned in polite novels by women: adultery, miscegenation, suicide. Her novels, like those of Charlotte Perkins Gilman, were infused with a sense of domestic entrapment and despair. In their sophistication and precise realism, they provide challenging parallels to the works of such male contemporaries as Stephen Crane, Jack London, and Frank Norris.

℘ Frances Ellen Watkins Harper
(1825–1911)

Iola Leroy, or, Shadows Uplifted.
Philadelphia: Garrigues, 1892
Columbia University, Rare Book and Manuscript Library

Frances Ellen Watkins Harper, born to a free, middle-class family in Maryland, was a well-known essayist and poet by the time *Iola Leroy,* her only novel, appeared in 1892. Like Phillis Wheatley a century earlier, she had run into difficulty finding a publisher for her earliest work, *Forest Leaves,* a collection of poetry now lost; but her second volume, *Poems on Miscellaneous Subjects* (1854), sold over 12,000 copies in the first four years after it was published, and by 1871 had been reprinted twenty-one times.

Harper was persuaded to write *Iola Leroy* in the 1890s when she was sixty-seven years old, largely because she felt that the much-praised writers of the New South, like Thomas Nelson Page and Joel Chandler Harris, were romanticizing slavery and its victims. She determined that a more accurate view of slavery should be offered to the readers of popular fiction. Her novel, the tale of a girl of mixed blood, articulates with great clarity the moral and intellectual issues that clustered around the question of race. Although occasionally awkward and inconsistent as a work of imaginative literature, its combination of intelligence and sentiment appealed to a diverse audience and helped to make Harper one of the best selling African-American writers of the nineteenth century.

᠀ Anna Julia Cooper
(1859–1964)

A Voice from the South: By a Black Woman of the South.
Xenia, OH: Aldine Printing House, 1892
The Library Company of Philadelphia

The daughter of a slave woman, Anna Julia Cooper lived into the era when the civil rights of African-Americans had once more moved into the center of American political and social culture. A teacher, writer, and educator who received an M.A. from Oberlin College in 1888 and later earned a Ph.D. in Latin literature from the Sorbonne, Anna Cooper was perhaps the most distinguished of the many black feminists whose articulate concern for their communities began to appear in print in the 1890s.

Cooper's novel, *A Voice from the South*, brought to public consciousness the distinct but related issues of gender, education, and race, and disputed with those who preferred to limit females to the domestic sphere, saying that "no woman can possibly put herself or her sex outside any of the interests that affect humanity."

᠀ Charlotte Perkins Stetson,
later
Charlotte Perkins Gilman
(1860–1935)

"The Yellow Wall-Paper."
New England Magazine, January 1892
Mary C. Schlosser

The Yellow Wall Paper.
Boston: Small, Maynard & Company, 1899
Barnard College, Overbury Collection

Women and Economics, A Study of the Economic Relation Between Men and Women as a Factor in Social Evolution.
Boston: Small, Maynard & Co., 1898
Mary C. Schlosser

Poet, lecturer, and author, Charlotte Gilman spent her life protesting against the economic impotence of women in society and trying to improve their status and opportunities, thus echoing her great-aunt Catharine Beecher. Great-niece also of Harriet Beecher Stowe and Henry Ward Beecher, she was the daughter of Frederick Beecher Perkins, who abandoned the family shortly after her birth, leaving her to a childhood of poverty. She attended the Rhode Island School of Design briefly (her only formal education), where she met Charles Walter Stetson, an artist whom she married in 1884. The birth of her only child, Catharine, in 1885 was followed by a post-natal breakdown, which continued intermittently until 1888 when the couple decided to separate and she went, alone, to stay with friends in California.

There she began to write for newspapers and magazines. An early effort was *The Yellow Wall Paper*, which appeared first as a magazine story and seven years later as a separate volume. Charlotte tells of a woman who has a nervous breakdown after childbirth, and her husband and physician insist that she isolate herself in the country for complete rest. She is not allowed to write or exercise any creative effort—though this is what she wants to do; she is driven mad by visions of a woman imprisoned behind the figured wallpaper in her bedroom. She tears the paper off the wall to liberate the woman, who is, of course, herself. Originally read as a Poe-esque tale of horror, this novella is now understood as Gilman's obviously autobiographical, vivid expression of rage against male domination.

Writing satirical poems and giving socialist speeches, she began to travel widely. She met Lester Ward, who was to be a great influence on her, at a suffrage meeting in Washington, D.C. Ward was the founder of sociology as a discipline in America, and believed that "male and female were equal in nature and that society had distorted their functions." In 1896 Charlotte went to England to the International Socialist and Labor Congress, where she was one of the few prominent women lecturers. On her return to the United States, she gathered her thoughts into *Women and Economics*, whose publication brought her instant fame. Widely reviewed, the *Nation* called it "the most significant utterance on the subject since Mill's *Subjection of Women*." The originality of Gilman's thinking lay in not blaming men for the subjugation of women, but arguing that society had slowly transformed from a time of equality of the sexes until women had become economic slaves. She believed that work had intrinsic value and was a means of identity, and that liberating women to work outside the home would benefit both men and women: ". . . whosoever, man or woman, lives always in a small dark place, is always guarded, protected, directed and restrained, will become inevitably narrowed and weakened by it."

Because of her controversial views, she had trouble getting her writings published, so in 1909 she started a monthly magazine, *The Forerunner*. Unassisted, she wrote the whole magazine (publishing in it four entire novels, including the utopian *Herland*) for seven years, despite constant financial difficulties. She continued to write and to give lectures and courses (some under James B. Pond's management), until her suffering from cancer drove her to suicide.

Despite the wide recognition of her social theories in the early years of the century, a turn to conservatism after World War I, and the pervasiveness of a big-business morality, turned Gilman's ideas aside. It was only with the republication of *Women and Economics* in 1966 and *Herland* in 1979 that her theories have begun to be reexamined and her importance as a precursor of today's feminism acknowledged.

❧ Katherine O'Flaherty Chopin, "Kate Chopin"

(1851–1904)

Bayou Folk.
Boston: Houghton, Mifflin, 1894
Barnard College, Overbury Collection

The Awakening.
Chicago: H. S. Stone & Co., 1899
An autograph letter to her publisher is pasted to the flyleaves of this copy.
University of Virginia, Taylor Collection of American Best-Sellers

Before Kate Chopin published her first piece of fiction, she had been married and widowed, and had borne six children. Educated in St. Louis, where she had grown up speaking French and English at home, Kate O'Flaherty moved first to New Orleans, and then to Natchitoches Parish in north-central Louisiana, after her marriage to a cotton factor, Oscar Chopin (pronounced "Choppin"). She moved back to St. Louis when Chopin died in 1883, and became active in the social and intellectual life of the city.

Chopin allocated only one or two days a week to her writing, claiming that it was important for her to participate in society in order to gain raw material for her fiction. She did read widely, particularly in modern French literature, and at first supported her family by translating popular works. Influenced by the technique and subject matter of her favorite writer, Guy de Maupassant, she demonstrated a more polished style and a more detached tone than was common among the American writers of her day.

Chopin's first novel, *At Fault*, appeared in 1890. Her short stories, collected first in *Bayou Folk*, were considered flowerings of the regional tradition, but it soon became clear that she had far broader interests than the usual local-color author, and a willingness to take risks in her treatment of race and of sexual taboos. Her best-known short story, "Desirée's Baby," a depiction of the consequences of miscegenation, betrays a deep bitterness and intense concern with female destinies. *The Awakening* tells the story of a disillusioned married society woman, who willingly steps outside the accepted social bounds to have an affair and is driven to suicide. Powerful and succinct, it addresses issues of individual autonomy and human fate with a compelling skill.

℘ Pauline Elizabeth Hopkins
(1859–1930)

Contending Forces: A Romance Illustrative of Negro Life North and South.
Boston: The Colored Cooperative Publishing Company, 1900
Yale University, Beinecke Library

Like Anna Julia Cooper, Frances Harper, and other African-American women who commanded public attention in the early years of the twentieth century, Pauline Hopkins spent much of her adult life publicly combating racial oppression. A strong black nationalist, she was, like her colleague W. E. B. DuBois, far enough removed from slavery to be impatient with unfulfilled promises.

Her most visible social role, one that links Hopkins to many of the other women in this exhibition, was as an editor and magazine writer. She was a member of the board of directors of *Colored American Magazine (CAM)*, the first significant twentieth-century African-American journal owned and published by blacks, and maintained throughout the early years of the century sufficient power to determine much of the editiorial content of the periodical. In *Contending Forces*, she used the conventions of sentimental romance—including hidden identities, amazing coincidences, and melodrama—to, in her own words, "raise the stigma of degradation from my race."

Bound for Glory
Modernism and the
New Bohemia

The modernist movement in American literature owed much of its success to the efforts of women, from Mabel Dodge Luhan and Gertrude Stein, in whose salons the conversation and talents of writers and artists were nurtured, to Harriet Monroe, whose periodical *Poetry,* introduced a whole new generation of poets to Americans. Women writers, often living in the new literary Bohemias of Greenwich Village, Provincetown, and Santa Fe, discarded not only the sometimes suffocating conventions of nineteenth-century social life, but also what they declared to be stifling literary forms. Women whose most important works belong to the 1920s, 1930s, and 1940s—Ellen Glasgow, Katherine Anne Porter, Marianne Moore—issued their earliest works in the teens, entering professional careers as writers with a confidence and zest that would have been envied by many of their predecessors.

The success of women playwrights like Susan Glaspell and Zona Gale was recognized by the all-male Pulitzer Prize advisory board, as well as by the enthusiastic audiences who gathered to applaud their plays. But it was really the accomplishments of Willa Cather, Gertrude Stein, and Edith Wharton—authors as different from one another as any in the American canon—that demonstrated the triumphant progress of the American woman author from the margins of literary achievement into the mainstream. While each of these created an uneven body of works and each made compromises of one sort or another, they all produced books which profoundly influenced the writers and readers of their own and subsequent generations.

Cather's best fiction is informed by the isolation of frontier life and the beauty of the natural world. Stein's works are marked by a playful sense of freedom from semantic and literary convention. Wharton's most serious novels elevate the niceties of domestic manners to the plane of high morality. Each is unmistakably American, but their words are at once feminine and without gender.

℘ Willa Sibert Cather
(1873–1947)

O Pioneers!
Boston & New York: Houghton Mifflin, 1913
Caroline F. Schimmel

My Ántonia. With Illustrations by W. T. Benda.
Boston & New York: Houghton Mifflin, 1918
This copy was inscribed "To Mrs. Goudy in memory of those optima dies. Willa Cather New York 1919." She had been Willa's high school principal in Red Cloud, Nebraska.
University of Virginia, C. Waller Barrett Collection

When Willa Cather was nine, her father, a Virginia farmer, uprooted his wife and growing family from his native state to southern Nebraska, eventually settling in the town of Red Cloud where he took to dealing in farm loans and mortgages. In Red Cloud, then a prairie outpost surrounded by frequently frozen and rainswept open spaces, young Willa, the eldest of seven, with cropped hair and dimples, and already considered eccentric by her family, came to know her similarly uprooted European neighbors. Mostly Swedes, Bohemians, and Poles, they struggled to exist on the alien, environmentally unwelcoming, and virtually treeless terrain, while being scorned by their American-born neighbors for their very foreignness. At sixteen, she entered the University of

Nebraska in Lincoln. There she embarked on a career of short-story writing and journalism, ending up in New York, and eventually serving as managing editor of *McClure's* magazine.

At last, in her thirties, with three fairly well-received novels, and a member of the New York literati, Cather had the money to travel both to Europe and to the newly fashionable Southwest. Although her first and true love, Isabelle McClung, had gotten married, leaving her bereft, another close friend, Sarah Orne Jewett, gave her the confidence to write full time. She resigned from *McClure's* in 1912, and devoted the rest of her life to writing fiction.

In general, the twelve novels and hundreds of short stories that Cather produced represent thematic variations on her own adolescent experience and those of her immigrant neighbors on the empty Nebraska plains and on a quintessential American experience: the search for a stability which, once achieved, proves to be illusionary and empty.

Ironically, as her fame increased, Cather's fictional skills declined. Her late works lack the freshness and deep sincerity which had characterized her earlier fiction. Her distrust of change, her innate conservatism, perhaps subsumed her creativity. Indeed, she felt so threatened by technological advances, she refused to have her work reproduced in any medium other than print. She announced that any author should be valued by his or her work alone, and demanded that all her correspondence be burned. As her popularity grew, so did her craving for simpler times, for solitude and peace. Yet she could not avoid the honors. She was awarded the Pulitzer Prize in 1922 for *One of Ours*, and throughout the 1930s received a spate of honorary degrees from such prestigious universities as Yale, Princeton, and Columbia. When she died at age seventy-three, she was one of the most beloved American authors of her era.

In *O Pioneers!* Cather praises repeatedly the value of "Old World" beliefs and folk remedies as the best tools to deal with the harsh land. Yet, contrary to old-world tradition, in this discouraging place only a woman, Alexandra Bergson, succeeds, because,

"For the first time, perhaps, since that land emerged from the waters of geologic ages, a human face was set toward it with love and yearning." The love affair, the erotic dreams, even the adultery and the murder that follows, are startlingly secondary to Alexandra's creation of a peaceable kingdom, the farm which is the true romance of the book. Cather dedicated the novel "To the memory of Sarah Orne Jewett in whose beautiful and delicate work there is the perfection that endures."

Many of Cather's most successful books are set in the immutable, mystical desert landscape of the Southwest that so fascinated her, but it is *My Àntonia*, set like *O Pioneers!* in the grasslands of the Midwest, that has been most beloved by her readers and most admired by critics in America and abroad. Written as the horrific war in Europe ended, Cather's book offered a bold sweeping terrain and a simpler time and culture as solace in an increasingly complex world. Although its ending is more romantic than would be true in later novels, the protagonists are recognizable, not larger than life, but ordinary people trying to exist in a bleak landscape that was nonetheless described with warmth as well as awe.

℘ Gertrude Stein
(1874–1946)

Three Lives: Stories of the Good Anna, Melanctha and the Gentle Lena.
New York: The Grafton Press, 1909
Barnard College, Overbury Collection

The Making of Americans, Being the History of a Family's Progress.
Paris: Published by Contact Editions, Three Mountain Press, 1925
Barnard College, Overbury Collection

The popularity of out-of-context phrases from the works of
Gertrude Stein—for example, the ubiquitous "A rose is a rose is a
rose"—tends to obscure the seriousness of her career and purpose.
As one recent critic has described it: "She wished only to be accurate, to record with precision those aspects of life that one could see
and hear." This too-brief summary still helps us begin to under-
stand the experimental nature of Stein's earliest published writings.
It also points to the influence on her work by the then upcoming
generation of Paris-based painters and sculptors (most notably
Pablo Picasso), whose concerns with linear surfaces and lines Stein
attempted to emulate in her writings.

Stein's marriage of linear surfaces and the written word proved
to be short-lived, and she was to turn in her later writings to a more
intelligible style. Her earlier prose nevertheless influenced a generation of aspiring American authors, including that most "mascu-
line" of writers, Ernest Hemingway, who was instrumental in
arranging for the publication in 1925 of Stein's so-called masterwork, *The Making of Americans*, written more than two decades
earlier. *Three Lives*, another early work which did not readily find
a publisher, is an unusually effective attempt to reflect the consciousness of three working-class women. Using a deliberately
simple and rhythmic language, the narrative is dominated by the
sad story of the African-America Melanctha Herbert.

Although she lived in Paris for most of her adult life, her language, themes, and subject matter remained resolutely American
and indisputably original. Her German-Jewish parents had emigrated to America when Stein was four. She was a magna cum
laude graduate of Radcliffe, where she was a favorite student of
William James, and attended Johns Hopkins Medical School for

two years. Her last completed work, was the libretto for Virgil Thomson's opera, *The Mother of Us All*, based on the life of Susan B. Anthony.

℘ Susan Glaspell,
later
Mrs. George Cram Cook
(1876–1948)

Trifles: A Play in One Act. Two typed drafts of the play, with typed and manuscript corrections, undated.
Shown are two versions of the final page of text, showing her extensive reworking of the lines.
New York Public Library, Berg Collection of English and American Literature

Trifles.
New York: Frank Shay; Washington Square Players, 1916
This copy is inscribed by the author on the cover: "Please return this copy as I have no other. The play is about to be republished by Small Maynard & Co. of Boston but I am anxious to buy a copy of this edition. S. G."
University of Virginia, C. Waller Barrett Collection

Like many of the innovative creators of American fiction and drama in the early years of the twentieth century, Susan Glaspell was born and educated in the Midwest. Although she began her career with the publication of a popular romance, *The Glory of the Conquered*, in 1909, her most acclaimed fictional works were to be her short stories, where the sharp details of everyday life used so effectively by earlier local-color writers were used to underscore a humanist philosophy and a feminist critique of small town life. One of her best stories is the much anthologized "A Jury of Her Peers" (1917), based on a murder case and trial on which Glaspell had reported in the Des Moines *Daily News*, where she had worked fifteen years before.

Glaspell moved East and became a vital part of the group of socially concerned writers and playwrights that included Floyd Dell, George Cram Cook, and Eugene O'Neill. She was responsible for inviting O'Neill into the dramatic organization she and Cook had organized in 1916, the Provincetown Players, for which she also wrote plays. *Trifles* is probably the best known of these. A one-act drama using the same material as "A Jury of Her Peers," *Trifles* is a strong feminist statement, and has been recently rediscovered, widely read, and even filmed for television. Glaspell's last novel, *Alison's House*, won the 1931 Pulitzer Prize.

℘ Zona Gale
(1874–1938)

Neighborhood Stories.
New York: The Macmillan Company, 1914
This copy is inscribed by the author to Mr. and Mrs. Orlando Ronlands, quoting the novel's heroine: "—right out there is the way life is, <u>when we can get it uncovered</u>."
Caroline F. Schimmel

Miss Lulu Bett.
New York & London: D. Appleton and Company, 1920
Barnard College, Overbury Collection

Miss Lulu Bett. An American Comedy of Manners.
New York & London: D. Appleton and Company, 1921
Barnard College, Overbury Collection

Carbon of a typed letter, signed by Frank D. Fackenthal for the Pulitzer Prize committee and Columbia University, dated May 26, 1921, and an autograph letter, by Zona Gale, written from Portage, Wisconsin, 11 June 1921.
The letter from Mr. Fackenthal describes her play as the one "which best represents the educational value and the power of the

stage in raising the standard of good morals, good taste and good manners." Her letter of thanks is brief, but filled with obvious delight.

Columbia University, School of Journalism

Zona Gale spent most of her adult life in the small town of Portage, Wisconsin. A popular novelist, her best works manage to shake off the sentimentalism that mars the weaker ones. In the fairly hackneyed *Neighborhood Stories*, a group of short pieces about a Midwestern town are linked by the appearance of our heroine, sensible, pious, liberal Calliope Marsh. She gently reprimands those who wish to keep housemaids in servitude, those who feel divorce from a faithless drunkard is shameful, and those who have lost the "little town" ability to join together to assist the downtrodden or to leaven grief with laughter. The book's publisher, with an eye to sales rather than text, decreed an irresistibly florid decorative lavender binding with lashings of color and gilt.

Gale published *Miss Lulu Bett* as a short novel. Its story of small town life and the sufferings of a spinster sister at the hands of her selfish family matched the taste of the reading public. It was, together with Sinclair Lewis's *Main Street*, the bestselling book of 1920. Gale's adaptation of the play for the stage, directed by William De Mille at the Belmont Theater, was equally successful, and the fact that she changed the script to give the work a happy ending some days after the opening did not prevent the Pulitzer jury from awarding her in May 1921 the annual $1,000 prize.

℘ Edith Newbold Jones Wharton
(1862–1937)

The House of Mirth.
New York: Charles Scribner and Sons, 1908

Columbia University, Rare Book and Manuscript Library, gift of Iola S. Haverstick

The Age of Innocence.
New York: Charles Scribner and Sons, 1920
This copy, in a special, elaborate tooled morocco binding by Gruel,
is inscribed by the author: "With admiration & gratitude to
Katherine Cornell, whose art has given new life to the wistful
ghost of Ellen Olenska. Edith Wharton July 1929." The actress was
than performing in *The Age of Innocence* on Broadway.

Columbia University, Rare Book and Manuscript Library, gift of Iola S. Haverstick

Carbons of two typed letters, signed by Frank D. Fackenthal for the
Pulitzer Prize committee and Columbia University, dated 26 May and
3 June 1921, and a typed letter, signed by Edith Wharton, dated
Pavillon Colombe, St Brice-sous-Forêt, France, 10 June 1921.
In contrast to the letter sent to Zona Gale, Mr. Fackenthal's to
Edith Wharton describes *The Age of Innocence* as the novel "which
best presents the wholesome atmosphere of American life and the
highest standard of American manners and manhood." He advises
her that the President of the University wishes to hand her the
check in person in Paris. We do not know if he did. Her response
is even briefer and more formal than Zona Gale's, an inkling of
how startled she was at being considered wholesome. Since the
prior winter, she had tried in vain to sell the short story "The Old
Maid" to any publisher, because the heroine has an illegitimate
child.

Columbia University, School of Journalism

By virtue of her socially prominent background, Edith Wharton
was to maintain and enjoy the status of "Grande Dame." She
also honed and polished her girlhood literary talent for writing,
to become, according to biographer R. W. B. Lewis, "the most
renowned writer in America." By the time she died at the age of
seventy-five, she had published forty-four books and was at work
on another, *The Buccaneers*, published posthumously in 1938.

Born Edith Newbold Jones in New York City, she married, at
the age of twenty-three, Edward ("Teddy") Wharton. Thirteen
years her senior, Wharton, who had been living with his mother

on an allowance of $2,000 a year, was an amiable, handsome man, but did not share her intellectual interests. The newly-weds decamped from Newport to a sumptuous mansion, the Mount, which they built in Lenox, Massachusetts and where they summered for the next ten years (wintering in Europe). They moved to France permanently in 1911, shortly before Teddy suffered a nervous collapse and was placed in a sanatorium. Divorced in 1913, Edith Wharton spent her remaining years in her adopted country where, independently wealthy thanks in part to the proceeds from her writings, she maintained houses outside of Paris and on the Riviera. Decorated by both the French and the Belgian governments for her World War I work on behalf of refugees and orphans, she was also lauded in her homeland for her writings, receiving honorary degrees from both Columbia and Yale, as well as the Pulitzer Prize for fiction.

In *The House of Mirth*, her first novel of manners, Wharton used the contemporary New York social scene as a background to contrast the strict moral values of the old Knickerbocker world of her childhood with the looser mores of an upcoming—and ultimately dominant—society whose newly-attained fortunes and consequent social prominence had, as novelist and literary critic Louis Auchincloss, put it, "changed the brownstone fronts of Fifth Avenue into a fantastic jumble of derivative palaces." Caught in the vortex between the two worlds is Wharton's heroine, the ill-fated and charming Lily Bart. Born and raised in the old New York world, but without inherited wealth and thus in need of a moneyed marriage, Lily flirts with the new society, only in the end to be rejected by both groups. A critical and popular success, *The House of Mirth* is distinguished not only by Wharton's dispassionate dissection of her subject matter, but also by a compelling and flowing style that was to become a hallmark of the author's prose.

Acknowledged as Wharton's masterwork, *The Age of Innocence* marked its author's successful return to the subject matter with which she seemed most at ease, namely the world of her early

New York background. Set in the 1870s, *The Age of Innocence* is essentially the story of its straight-laced upper-class hero, Newland Archer, and his pre- and post-marital infatuation with the glamorous Countess Ellen Olenska, his wife's cousin. Socially suspect because she has fled from her European husband under seemingly mysterious circumstances, Ellen is similarly attracted to Archer but ultimately graciously retreats. The novel's poignant denouement is a fitting tribute to Wharton's skills as both story-teller and writer.

ᘏ Authors by Date of Birth

1612?–1672, Anne Dudley Bradstreet
1635?–1678?, Mary White Rowlandson
1666–1727, Sarah Kemble Knight
1728–1814, Mercy Otis Warren
1753?–1784, Phillis Wheatley
1759–1855, Sarah Barrell Wood
1762–1824, Susanna Haswell Rowson
1769–1853, Anne Newport Royall
1788–1879, Sarah Josepha Hale
1789–1867, Catharine Maria Sedgwick
1791–1865, Lydia Howard Sigourney
1792–1873, Sarah Moore Grimké
1800–1856, Caroline Lee Hentz
1800–1878, Catharine Esther Beecher
1801–1864, Caroline Matilda Stansbury
  Kirkland
1802–1880, Lydia Maria Francis Child
1804–1894, Elizabeth Palmer Peabody
1805–1879, Angelina Emily Grimké
1806–1887, Mary Tyler Peabody Mann
1810–1850, Sarah Margaret Fuller,
  Marchesa d' Ossoli
1811–1872, Sara Payson Willis Parton
1811–1896, Harriet Beecher Stowe
1813–1897, Harriet Ann Jacobs
1815–1902, Elizabeth Cady Stanton
1819–1885, Susan Bogert Warner
1819–1899, Emma Dorothy Eliza Nevitte
  Southworth
1820–1871, Alice Cary
1820–1900, Lucretia Peabody Hale
1820–1906, Susan Brownell Anthony
1823–1904, Sara Jane Clarke Lippincott
1825?–1870?, Harriet E. Adams Wilson
1825–1911, Frances Ellen Watkins Harper
1827–1866, Maria Susanna Cummins
1830–1885, Helen Hunt Jackson
1830–1886, Emily Dickinson
1830–1905, Mary Mapes Dodge
1831–1910, Rebecca Harding Davis
1832–1888, Louisa May Alcott

1833–1896, Mary Abigail Dodge
1834–1915, Abigail Duniway
1834–1915, Annie Adams Fields
1835–1894, Celia Laighton Thaxter
1835–1905, Sarah Chauncey Woolsey
1835–1909, Augusta Jane Evans Wilson
1837–1914, Charlotte L. Forten
1840–1894, Constance Fenimore
  Woolson
1842–1928, Ina Donna Coolbrith
1844–1891, Sarah Winnemucca Hopkins
1844–1911, Elizabeth Stuart Phelps Ward
1844–1924, Harriet Stone Lothrop
1846–1935, Anna Katharine Green Rohlfs
1849–1887, Emma Lazarus
1849–1909, Sarah Orne Jewett
1849–1924, Frances Hodgson Burnett
1850–1922, Mary Noailles Murfree
1851–1904, Katherine O'Flaherty Chopin
1851–1931, Ida Husted Harper
1852–1930, Mary Eleanor Wilkins
  Freeman
1857–1948, Gertrude Horn Atherton
1859–1930, Pauline Elizabeth Hopkins
1859?–1964, Anna Julia Cooper
1860–1935, Charlotte Perkins Stetson
  Gilman
1860–1936, Harriet Monroe
1862–1937, Edith Newbold Jones
  Wharton
1868–1934, Mary Hunter Austin
1871–1940, Bertha Muzzy Sinclair Cowaɪ
1873–1947, Willa Sibert Cather
1874–1925, Amy Lowell
1874–1938, Zona Gale
1874–1946, Gertrude Stein
1876–1948, Susan Glaspell
1886–1961, Hilda Doolittle

Index